THE GOOD OL' BOYS

by

DENNIS CONROY

Order this book online at www.trafford.com/08-1025
or email orders@trafford.com

Most Trafford titles are also available at major online book retailers.

Note for Librarians: A cataloguing record for this book is available from Library and Archives Canada at www.collectionscanada.ca/amicus/index-e.html

ISBN: 978-1-4251-8515-2

We at Trafford believe that it is the responsibility of us all, as both individuals and corporations, to make choices that are environmentally and socially sound. You, in turn, are supporting this responsible conduct each time you purchase a Trafford book, or make use of our publishing services. To find out how you are helping, please visit www.trafford.com/responsiblepublishing.html

Our mission is to efficiently provide the world's finest, most comprehensive book publishing service, enabling every author to experience success. To find out how to publish your book, your way, and have it available worldwide, visit us online at www.trafford.com/10510

www.trafford.com

North America & international
toll-free: 1 888 232 4444 (USA & Canada)
phone: 250 383 6864 • fax: 250 383 6804
email: info@trafford.com

The United Kingdom & Europe
phone: +44 (0)1865 487 395 • local rate: 0845 230 9601
facsimile: +44 (0)1865 481 507 • email: info.uk@trafford.com

10 9 8 7 6 5 4 3 2 1

THE GOOD OL' BOYS

by

DENNIS CONROY

Also Published.
By the same author:

"The Cairo Connection"	Fiction
"The Best of Luck"	Non-Fiction
"Back Seat Specialist"	Non-Fiction
"Collie"	Non-Fiction
"Second Sight"	Fiction
"Dogs of War"	Non-Fiction

THANKS

To my wife Patricia for her constant support during my writing of "The Good Ol' Boys".

For her checking of the text and her suggestions for improvement of the book.

ACKNOWLEDGMENT

The picture of the Thompson submachine gun on the front cover of this book was taken from TheFreeDictionary.com by Farlex Inc.USA.

The picture of the UZI submachine gun on the rear cover of this book was taken from WIKIPEDIA The Free Encyclopedia.

NOTE

Many characters in this book are based on real life individuals. However, to save embarrassment, or worse, names have been changed especially where the criminal element is concerned.

Author Biographical Note

Dennis Conroy, a World War 2 veteran, served as air-gunner and fighter pilot in the Royal Air Force, being attached briefly to the United States 8th. Air Force in Great Britain.

Later Dennis Conroy had a variegated career including president of a self-owned group of companies, civil servant, bodyguard with a major international security group and market research statistician, among others.

In spite of this variety of occupations Dennis Conroy wrote short stories and articles for magazines and newspapers continually. So continually that his first article was published in 1938 and the latest in 2008 thus surely making him one of the longest published writers today.

Apart from six years of warfare Dennis Conroy has fought crime in a civilian capacity. During a long employment as Security Officer in an international retail company he worked in close co-operation with the Criminal Investigation Department of a large police force. Here he instigated numerous arrests of organized criminals many reacting violently when apprehended. On one occasion both he and his opponent were hospitalized. Luckily Dennis Conroy was granted a monetary award by higher authority for injuries received. Higher authority also awarded the criminal a hefty jail sentence.

Dennis Conroy lived for many years in the Middle East and learned much about the international mafia running drugs through Egypt to Europe. He knew and socialized with many police officers, European and Egyptian, who were involved in combating the drug barons.

Dennis Conroy now lives peacefully on Vancouver Island, Canada

"THE GOOD OL' BOYS" by DENNIS CONROY

GUIDE TO CONTENTS

GUIDE TO CONTENTS
(continued)

GUIDE TO CONTENTS
(continued)

PREAMBLE

From "THE CAIRO CONNECTION" by Dennis Conroy

* * * * *

About mid-September 1963 Luigi had a call from Santos Salvatore.

All communications between us and our contacts in the United States were directed to Luigi personally because, I guessed, he was a mafia Don.

It seemed that Santos wanted a business discussion on an important matter and he requested the presence of our four senior members, Otto Guynemer, Luigi Ferraro, Angelo Rizzoli and me, Deacon Roy.

He intimated, discreetly, that no ladies should accompany us.

So off to Miami, Florida, we flew, hoping that the important matter under discussion was not going to be the reduction of our drug shipments.

We met Santos Salvatore initially in a pent-house on a condominium at Miami Beach.

Judging by the furnishings it was obviously one of his minor appurtenances probably used mainly for private discussions.

Two very polite but exceedingly tough looking bodyguards escorted us into the presence and then retired to the entrance.

Santos was affable but unusually contemplative. I could tell that he had something serious on his mind. After a short bout of introductory chit-chat he came very strongly to the point but with some degree of caution.

He took command and started, "I'm asking you guys, point blank, to do an important hit job for me and for the benefit of the rest of Cosa Nostra in America. Only two other top mafiosi, Carlos Mancini of New Orleans and Jo Fratello of Chicago, know I'm approaching you on this matter.

There's no need to tell you fellows that absolute secrecy is essential. You already know not to mention one word of this discussion outside these walls to wives, family or whoever."

PREAMBLE (Continued)

A brief pause.

And then, "This target is going to be hit! But the hit must be professional and final!"

He paused again, took a drink of water from a conveniently placed glass and held up a firm hand to stop me butting in with a question.

"Let me finish speaking." he admonished quietly. So we waited while he quenched his thirst and lit a cigar.

He continued, "I don't intend to mention the name of our target but I will tell why we have asked you three guys to pull the triggers."

He indicated Luigi, Angelo and me with a broad sweep of his hand, finger pointing.

His serious face lit up with a short sort of grin as he stated, "First we have a very good idea of your hit record in several countries. Even we in America have heard of the Marseilles and Paris massacres, to name but two!"

He carried on, "We need experienced hit men who are crack shots with all weapons, especially high-powered rifles.

We do not want to use triggermen from America as, after the hit, we want the shooters to apparently vanish from the face of the earth.

That means using men from overseas and you guys can return to Europe at short notice and thus avoid any risk of discovery by the law.

If you guys can do this job successfully you need never worry again about your business affairs in the United States.

You will be in good and solid with me and my two leading colleagues, Jo and Carlos. No one else will ever know your names in connection with this job."

He halted for a short second and looked directly at each one of us in rapid sequence.

Then straight out and abruptly he asked, "Will you guys consider doing this job?"

Another pause and then, "I'd be happy if you told me, one way or the other, before you leave here to-day."

He rose to his feet suddenly, adding, "I'm going to leave you alone to talk the matter over. When you want me back

PREAMBLE (continued)

just open the door and yell!"

At that he quit the room and shut the door.

Luigi took the floor immediately.

"We've got to do this job," he said, "we are too deeply involved with the Americans, financially and organizationally, to balk at this one. And remember, our cartel is Cosa Nostra and our United States involvement is with Cosa Nostra. We must work together for the benefit of all."

Then as Otto Guynemer nodded his agreement, Luigi asked for my comments.

I had no hesitation in stating we should do the hit.

Luigi smiled at my response, inquiring no further because our other member, Angelo, was a born mafioso anyway.

He strode to the door, opened it and bawled, "Santos!"

Salvatore joined us promptly, looking at us all expectantly.

"Well?" he queried.

Luigi's response was brief and to the point, "We are in, what now?"

The mafia boss soon told us what was coming next.

He said, "Tomorrow I'm going to New Orleans to discuss our plans with Carlos Mancini and Jo Fratello, I want you to come with me, Luigi, to join in the discussion.

You are a Don of high standing and are acceptable to my friends.

Now you have agreed to do the job it is essential for you to learn the details.”

He looked at us gravely, unsmilingly, and continued, "The rest of you can stay here in Miami and amuse yourselves.

When Luigi returns he can fill you all in about who's being hit and where.”

We shook hands and quit the pent-house.

* * * * *

PREAMBLE (ending)

Luigi spent three days in New Orleans hobnobbing with the top United States crime bosses.

It appeared that he resided during that period in one of Mancini's luxurious estates where he learned their future plans.

On his return we all met him at Miami International Airport and eagerly asked him the obvious questions.

He would disclose nothing.

Hardly a word was uttered until we drove well out of town in our rented Chrysler convertible.

We parked near the water in quasi-everglade country where Luigi considered there were no listening ears except those of the occasional semi-dormant alligator.

I started the interrogation by asking abruptly, "Who we gonna hit, Luigi?!"

Luigi responded smilingly, "Before I tell you the target I wanna emphasize that the main planning has been done already.

They've even indoctrinated a young jerk who's gonna be the unwitting fall-guy, the patsy who's unaware he's gonna take the blame for our hit!"

I burst in on his monologue impatiently, "It all sounds great, Luigi, but who the hell are we gonna hit?!"

Luigi's smile tightened as he quietly replied,

"Deac, it's a guy called JFK !"

* * * * *

CHAPTER ONE

PLANNING THE BIG ONE

After the initial shock of being told the name of the proposed victim had worn off we were put in the picture by Luigi in great detail.

The hit was to take place in Dallas, Texas, on November 22nd 1963 when JFK was paying the state an official visit.

I learned that the four of us, Otto Guynemer, Luigi Ferraro, Angelo Rizzoli and me, Deacon Roy, were visiting Dallas individually to check the layout of the killing zone and, incidentally, to meet Jack Rubenstein, a Jewish mobster originally sent to Dallas as contact man by the Chicago syndicate, who was known to have close contacts with many members of the local police force and associated law officers.

Our discussions with this individual were to be surreptitious, or at least as secretive as possible under the circumstances.

In view of the enormity of this murderous project each one of us involved in the actual shooting was issued with a pseudonym by Santos Salvatore, boss of the Cosa Nostra in Florida, who was currently based in Miami and was one of the two leading instigators of the planned assassination.

From now on each alias was used in any communications between those in the plot, our real identities being known only to Santos Salvatore and his fellow conspirator Carlos Mancini, boss of the New Orleans Cosa Nostra family.

* * * * *

Otto Guynemer was the first of our group to visit the Dallas area. He, of course, had planned most of the spectacular executions of our opponents in crime since our Cairo days and long before that when he worked as "business consultant" with the Capone syndicate in Chicago. During this latter period he, together with Luigi Ferraro, were suspected of major involvement and planning of the infamous St. Valentine's Day Massacre.

Guynemer decided to bunk in Fort Worth at the Hotel Texas. From here he could visit Dallas by car as and when he felt it necessary.

He surveyed the proposed presidential route through Dallas at his leisure and soon discovered that the most effective point for the assassination attempt would be where the presidential car turned left from Houston Street into Elm Street.

This left turn being a ninety degree "dog-leg" would ensure a reduced speed in all the cars in the procession, making it that much easier for the shooters to line up their telescopic sights on the target.

Further careful study of the selected site convinced him that his three experienced gunmen should be in two separate locations close enough to the cavalcade to ensure that the target was hit by each of them.

His chosen locations were the Texas School Book Depository building and a fence connecting a concrete pergola with the railroad overpass. The fence was on a grassy knoll and would be to the right of the motorcade when it passed that point.

The initial conjecture was to put one gunman in the Texas School Book Depository and both the others behind the fence on the grassy knoll.

Apart from the assassination Guynemer's other concern was to make sure the shooters could escape after the event.

It was obvious that a successful killing would turn a comparatively peaceful atmosphere into a tumultuous uproar, even a panic stricken shambles, and this could be conducive to a successful getaway by his men.

Guynemer decided to consult with Santos Salvatore about the best method of gaining access to the Texas School Book Depository at the required time and, incidentally, how to get the gunman away after he had fired his lethal shots.

* * * * *

Guynemer arranged to meet his Dallas contact man, Rubenstein, at a convenient restaurant not far from Fort Worth.

He had no wish to be seen in the company of Rubenstein by snooping eyes in Dallas.

His chief concern with Rubenstein was to ascertain the attitudes of certain local police officers and their reaction to the planned assassination.

Guynemer was relieved to discover that the senior police officers "in the know" already had the description of the patsy who was going to be blamed for the presidential slaughter and would have that description broadcast on police channels immediately after the event.

So while the majority of patrolmen were seeking the wrong person the escape of the actual gunmen would be simplified.

Also it was known by certain police officers that the patsy, named Oswald, had purchased a Mannlicher-Carcano rifle by mail order and it was intended that this firearm would be "discovered" by investigators at the apt time and most incriminating place.

* * * * *

Highly pleased with his initial survey of the proposed killing zone Guynemer flew back to Miami and discussed his findings with Luigi, Angelo and me.

He explained his ideas with the aid of detailed street maps and we decided which of us would shoot from which location.

It was agreed that Luigi would shoot from the Texas School Book Depository, probably from the west end of the fifth or sixth floor.

To reduce the time factor he would fire no more than two shots from his Mauser 7.65 mm rifle before dropping the gun and beating a hurried retreat from the building.

It would be essential for Luigi to wear thin plastic surgical gloves to avoid finger printing the weapon but this should not affect his accuracy.

He would also be equipped with false documentation showing he was a Secret Service agent if anybody queried his presence in the building. It was common knowledge that the Secret Service placed armed snipers in high buildings to protect presidential motorcades.

Luigi, on leaving the building, would be met by Jack Rubenstein, the guy with much local knowledge, and then take off in Rubenstein's car to be dropped near another car on the Fort Worth highway.

Luigi would then drive this vehicle to Fort Worth airport and fly to Miami.

Angelo and I were to shoot from behind the fence between the pergola and the railroad overpass. We were scheduled to fire one shot each from comparatively short range and immediately make for our getaway car, parked close by, and leave the area taking our Mauser rifles with us.

The driver of our getaway vehicle would be a man detailed by the Cosa Nostra and he would drop us off on the highway to Fort Worth where we would pick up yet another car, which had been left ready for us, and drive to Fort Worth airport, here we would leave the car and take off on a flight back to Miami.

It would not matter if we were on the same flight as Luigi because we were all acting independently and would not be conversing with each other until we reached safety. This individual attitude was insisted on by Guynemer as an extra security function.

* * * * *

Luigi was the next of our bunch of conspirators to survey the proposed killing area in Dallas. He too, on Guynemer's suggestion, stayed at a Fort Worth hotel and drove to Dallas at his convenience.

It was now the early days of November and Luigi was rather surprised, after externally checking the Texas School Book Depository, to learn from his routine discussion with Rubenstein that the patsy, Oswald, was actually working in the Depository as a laborer.

Luigi asked Rubenstein if there was any possibility of him being able to survey the interior of the Depository as he wanted to ascertain the most suitable position for his brief attack on the President. He conjectured this could be on the fifth or sixth floor and he wished to check access to and ways to exit from these floors, the most suitable window to shoot from and so on.

Luigi, like Guynemer, believed in planning assassinations in detail, leaving nothing to chance that could be foreseen.

Hence his numerous successful fatal hits. Fatal to his victims, that is!

Rubenstein answered Luigi's query by saying that he knew the supervisor at the Book Depository and would see what could be arranged.

At a subsequent meeting Jack Ruby (As Rubenstein was known in Dallas) told Luigi that he had arranged with the supervisor for Luigi to visit the building just after the finish of work on any day that suited him.

The foreman in charge at that time of day had been instructed to give Luigi access to the fifth and sixth floors.

Jack Ruby added that the supervisor had been informed Luigi was a newspaper man who wanted to check the suitability of the floors in question for taking photographs of the presidential motorcade.

Ruby was quite proud of his subterfuge but was subdued somewhat when Luigi forcibly emphasized that he did not want to be seen in Ruby's company in Dallas. This was an obvious security precaution but Luigi felt that Jack Ruby considered it a blow to his popularity!

Not that Luigi was concerned about Ruby's personal feelings as, in fact, he did not like the guy even though he had only met him a couple of times.

However, Luigi considered Ruby was reliable due to the fact that he had been recommended by Santos Salvatore, a man who had the power of life and death over the associates under his control.

Luigi had no problem visiting the Book Depository and checking the floors in which he was interested. He decided eventually to shoot from a window at the west end of the sixth floor.

Having made this decision Luigi had a look at the fence on the grassy knoll where Angelo and I were being placed. He made a few mental points concerning this location and proposed to pass his ideas on to us.

Angie and I could consider Luigi's suggestions when we made our exploratory visits to Dallas.

After his decisive stay in Dallas Luigi drove back to Fort Worth, spent the night in his hotel and, next morning, taxied to the airport and took the first available flight to Miami.

* * * * *

Before leaving Fort Worth Luigi had 'phoned Guynemer to inform him of his expected time of arrival in Miami.

Not wishing to attract undue attention the four members of our European cartel were staying in separate hotels so Otto Guynemer 'phoned Luigi's arrival time to Angelo and me. It was arranged that I would meet Luigi at the Airport and we would taxi to a café at Miami Beach where Luigi would discuss his trip with the rest of us.

* * * * *

Luigi explained the salient features which he had considered during his Dallas visit.

Positions behind the fence on the grassy knoll for Angelo and me plus Luigi's site in the Texas School Book Depository gave the three of us almost point-blank shots at our target.

Luigi emphasized, with Otto Guynemer's agreement, that we should shoot individually.

"Shoot at will when you have the best view of your target", he insisted and continued, " Don't wait for each other to fire first, remember the target is moving. The least delay and it will be out of range very rapidly."

Adding, "We haven't come over from Sicily to waste our goddamned time!"

Continuing, with just a hint of malicious sarcasm, " And we don't wanna upset Santos Salvatore and his buddies, do we?!"

He grinned as he asked this superfluous question.

We chuckled in response because, knowing Luigi over a long period, we were all well aware that he didn't worry about upsetting anybody if he thought they deserved it.

Both Luigi and Otto Guynemer suggested that Angelo and I should visit Dallas together and study the situation behind the fence, our proposed firing area.

Luigi mentioned, " You guys may find the fence is a bit too high for comfort. It's possible you will both need to stand on something in order to take careful aim. I noticed during my visit to the site that there were cars regularly parked close to the fence, some belonging to the local sheriff's department!"

Luigi paused with a grin then added, " It may be convenient for each of you to stand on a car bumper while you make your shots. Make sure you try doing that during your visit and let me know how you feel about it. On the big day it will be for a very short time so you won't be suffering for long!"

His jocular finish did not preclude the fact that his suggestion was an order. We were very much aware that Luigi and Otto were still the bosses of our cartel.

Otto intimated that there was no need for me and Angie to contact Jack Ruby during our visit. Luigi nodded agreement and remarked, " The fewer people that know our complete plan the fewer the mouths to blab after we make our hit. What Santos Salvatore tells Jack Ruby is his business but we won't tell him too much as I feel Jack could crack up if heavy judicial pressure was applied as I am certain it will be after the shooting."

After a few more minor points were raised and answered our café meeting broke up but not before Angelo and I were told to take off for Dallas the next day.

* * * * *

We both booked in at the Texas Hotel in Fort Worth. The management thought we were business visitors which, in fact, we were, although our business was rather unusual.

A hire car sped us to Dallas, driven by Angelo. It was parked conveniently near Dealey Plaza and we had a long survey of the proposed killing zone.

Luigi's selected site in the Texas School Book Depository was noted and we surveyed the area behind the fence on the grassy knoll in detail.

It was ideal for almost point-blank shots at the presidential motorcade and as Angelo remarked, " To miss our target at this range we would have to be skew-eyed, Deac, but I guess we'll have to stand on a couple of car bumpers to reach over that fence."

We felt the car bumper problem would be insignificant because, even as we watched, vehicles were parked and being parked the whole length of the fence. As Luigi had noted several of them were from the Sheriff's department!

Our brief presence on the coming 22nd November would be shielded from inquisitive eyes by some trees planted along part of the fence.

I noticed a railroad watch tower up on the overpass bridge so I mentioned, "Angie, the guy in that tower is probably the only person who will detect movement behind the fence, Whad'ya think about that?

Angelo's response was, " I guess the trees will hide us as we fire our shots and he might see us make our getaway but it should be too rapid movement for him to notice anything important. All we gotta do is make sure we wear gear that won't dazzle the eyeballs of the guys on the bridge. Otherwise they will tell the cops what the shooters wore and we don't want to risk that, do we, Deac?"

It was a small risk but I tacitly agreed with Angelo.

We stayed a couple of more days pondering about our future hit and familiarizing ourselves with Dealey Plaza and the streets leading to and from.

Our confidence was reinforced by our inspection in Dallas so we took off from Fort Worth airport, en route to Miami, in very good humor.

On top of which Otto and Luigi complimented us on the details in our report.

* * * * *

CHAPTER TWO

HOW WE DID THE BIG ONE
November 22, 1963

Angelo Rizzoli opened fire first, an easy shot at comparatively short range.

He knew very rapidly that he had hit the President because, through his telescopic sight, he saw JFK grasp his throat and slump back in his seat. All this before the Mauser rifle kicked back in recoil.

Immediately after firing this one successful shot Angie jumped off the car bumper on which he had been standing. This perch was necessary to allow him to shoot over the fence on the grassy knoll.

* * * * *

The next shot which quickly followed was fired by Luigi Ferraro, shooting through the left hand window on the sixth floor of the Texas School Book Depository.

At the precise moment that Luigi squeezed the Mauser trigger his target, the President, slumped to one side due to reaction to Angelo's throat shot. So, unfortunately, Luigi's first bullet hit the Governor of Texas, John Connally, who was riding in the presidential car.

Cursing at this inopportune occurrence Luigi reactivated the beautifully smooth bolt action of his 7.65 mm Mauser and shoved another cartridge up the spout. With little delay he fired again and, this time, hit his real target in the back.

Having succeeded in his task Luigi dropped the rifle, still loaded, and exited the building by the rear stairs and the back door.

* * * * *

I was the last guy to shoot. I am Deacon Roy and my shot was not difficult. I had JFK's head lined up in my 'scope and when I squeezed the trigger that is just where my bullet hit him.

The result was visually quite ghastly and I leapt off the car bumper where I was standing and joined Angelo in fleeing for our pick-up car.

* * * * *

The car, a mud be-spattered Chevrolet driven by a dedicated Cosa Nostra member, was waiting for us so we jumped in rapidly with our rifles and took off hastily as, already, patrolmen were climbing over the fence on the grassy knoll.

As we took off I noticed a car which appeared to be following us. Somewhat concerned I mentioned this to Angelo who watched the follower closely and discerned a middle-aged driver accompanied by a child. We soon lost this "follower" so guessed we were worrying over nothing.

In spite of the traffic shambles in Dealey Plaza we managed, by forceful driving, to maneuver our way to our vehicle on the road to Fort Worth, which had been left ready for us, and, leaving the Chevrolet, used our latest transport to drive to Fort Worth airport and book passages to Miami.

* * * * *

Luigi, having quit the Book Depository by the rear door, met our Dallas contact man, Jack Rubenstein, as planned and walked with him along Elm street, through the semi-hysterical crowd, until they reached the inconspicuous station wagon which was, in fact, Luigi's get-away car.

This wagon, complete with selected Cosa Nostra driver, transported Luigi to the Fort Worth highway where he too picked up yet another vehicle which he personally drove to Fort Worth airport and booked his flight to Miami.

* * * * *

Once back in Miami we went to our respective hotels where we packed our gear and booked out.

We did not leave our hotels immediately but loitered in the bars until we had our expected 'phone message from Otto Guynemer. He had been in touch with Santos Salvatore, who was delighted with the news of our successful hit, and instructed us to head for Miami airport to book our flights out of the United States.

I was booking to Marseilles, France as I intended to return to my residence in Corsica and the welcoming arms of my wife Firdaussi.

Luigi and Angelo were heading for Rome, Italy and then on to Syracuse in Sicily where they would pick up a car for the fifty mile trip to the grand estate which was the headquarters of Luigi's mafia cartel. There Don Luigi would meet his wife Tania and no doubt enjoy a loving homecoming.

Angelo's residence was in close proximity to Luigi's impressive home. Angelo, of course was the underboss of the large mafia family which controlled a large area of Eastern Sicily. In other words he was No. 2 man to Don Luigi.

He was looking forward to meeting his wife Maria.

I am sure it will be of interest to newcomers to this unusual tale to learn that Firdaussi, my Persian wife; Tania, Luigi's Turkish wife and Maria, Angelo's Italian wife were all ex-prostitutes!

My marriage led the way during our hectic years based in Cairo, Egypt where our violent group was in virtual control of the Middle East narcotics trade under the expert guidance of Otto Guynemer.

I must add that the three ladies in question proved to be faithful and loving spouses. Whether their past experiences urged them to partake of the finer things in life or whether the sudden influx of great wealth played a part it is hard to say.

As a closing note on the marriage state it should be emphasized that the three ladies were all well aware of the source of their wealth and were under no illusions regarding the employment class of their husbands!

* * * * *

When Guynemer 'phoned us at our Miami hotels, telling us to take off for Europe we all knew that he would not be joining us.

He had conferred with Santos Salvatore and requested him to sanction an introduction to the boss of one of the five New York Cosa Nostra families.

This family, headed by one Joseph Bonanno, had more than a passing interest in the functions of Sicilian mafia members based in Montreal, Canada; functions involving the narcotics traffic and large-scale money-laundering.

As our own drug deliveries were smuggled through New Brunswick, Canada before carting them to Maine, United States, Otto Guynemer wished to contact the Montreal mob and find out if it would be more efficient (and save money!) should we chose to pass our loads of narcotics through Montreal en route to USA via Windsor and Detroit. Or through Montreal to New York via Buffalo.

Jo Bonanno in New York, knowing that Otto Guynemer had been recommended by Santos Salvatore was very affable and once he knew Otto's intentions soon gave his OK and suggested who he should contact in Montreal.

The Montreal contact was Vincenzo Cotillo head of the family which collaborated very closely with the Bonannos of New York.

Otto Guynemer stayed a couple of weeks in Montreal and discussed drug matters extensively with Cotillo. There seemed to be few problems connected with handling our large supplies of narcotics, mainly heroin, and after delivery to Montreal our consignments would be transported to New York by the Bonanno/Cotillo organization. This would relieve our cartel of the present necessity of smuggling our shipments over the USA/Canada border, a dangerous, time consuming and expensive operation.

Pleased with his successful initial discussions Otto Guynemer made further personal contacts with the leading criminal element in the Quebec area.

He was impressed with one of Cotillo's associates, a Sicilian mafioso named Nicolo Rizzoli, who appeared to have his own ideas about the organization of the drug traffic through Montreal.

A man worth having on our side, thought Otto as he pondered on his visit while preparing for his return to Europe.

He also wondered if the Montreal Rizzoli was related to our Angelo Rizzoli, long time member of our cartel and, of course, the first of our shooters to hit JFK in the Dallas affair.

* * * * *

Guynemer decided to go directly to Sicily in order to pass on his Canadian experience to Luigi and the rest of us.

As Firdaussi and I were domiciled in Corsica, currently checking on our French business, based chiefly in Marseilles and Paris, Otto 'phoned us and instructed us to go to Sicily immediately.

We went in our usual fashion; by hired aircraft to Rome then by regular airline to Catania in Sicily where a car was waiting to pick us up, driven yet again by our old comrade-in-arms Angelo Rizzoli.

He sped us to Luigi's grand old manor, not far from the little town of Palazzolo, which had been home to the Ferraro family for many generations.

Angelo skidded to a halt in the gated courtyard and we were welcomed by Luigi and Tania accompanied by Angelo's wife Maria. Everybody seemed to be hugging and kissing, shaking hands and talking in loud voices. We were all glad to see each other again! Especially after the recent sanguine event in Dallas, Texas.

After a convivial drink or two we were shown to our room where we showered and cleaned up ready for the excellent dinner which followed. The three ladies had always got on well together and had plenty to talk about during and after the meal.

Their similar early backgrounds seemed to cement their

friendships even though their circumstances had changed dramatically since meeting the Good Ol' Boys during the Cairo era.

Luigi, Angelo and I had a great chin-wag over our brandy and cigars. We had plenty to talk about not having had the opportunity to discuss our recent adventures, as a threesome, in private.

Luigi, being one of the most powerful mafia Dons in Sicily had what was initially a local political problem. At a meeting of the chief Cosa Nostra Dons, including Luigi, a couple of years before in the island capital, Palermo, it had been suggested that a mafia commission should be set up. This organization would endeavor to keep "law and order" among the mafia families and arbitrate peaceful solutions to any disputes between families.

This was a good idea in some ways but Don Luigi had always tended to settle important disagreements in the traditional mafia fashion by applying a violent solution!

So he did not want interference in his family affairs, including letting the so-called commission know the detailed structure of our very large narcotics system in Europe and the United States.

He agreed to the commission setting up a small branch in Siracusa as was done in every other province in Sicily. However, Siracusa, the town, was not far from home so Luigi and his men could keep an overt eye on the couple of small-timers based there, the latter passing their useless time in enforced idleness as they knew that Don Luigi "owned" the area.

During my conversation with Luigi and Angelo it was obvious they only paid lip service to the commission scheme because Don Luigi Ferraro was confident in his own ability and did not need an organized commission to help his cartel's progress.

The snag was that the Corleone family, led by boss Bernardo Pacelli, considered they were the big shots and intended to run the commission to their own advantage, not excluding the use of violence and murder to further their ambitions.

Bernardo Pacelli was aware of Luigi's power and reputation and Luigi himself was aware that Pacelli had decided tentatively to eliminate Luigi and his senior cohorts, including Angelo.

So the initial political problem was fast becoming a power struggle.

Luigi told me directly, " We're gonna have to do something final to Pacelli and the Corleone mob, Deac, because the Ferraro family have always ruled this province and we don't intend to have a bunch of peasants muscling in on our patch!"

I knew for sure that Luigi's use of the term "we" included me. I had worked with the cartel for a long period and was very much one of the Good Ol' Boys!

Angelo drove off again next day to pick up Otto Guynemer at the airport.

Otto was welcomed enthusiastically by all and, after a clean up and a good lunch, soon settled down to a discussion of the problem imposed by Bernardo Pacelli and the Corleone mob.

Further, he put us in the picture about his visit to Canada. His impression was that we should use the current groups in Montreal to push our massive shipments of narcotics down to New York, possibly to the Bonanno family.

He explained his reasons for thinking on these lines and suggested to Luigi that Deac (me!) and Firdaussi should stay in Montreal and make the initial business negotiations with the selected Cosa Nostra leaders. Angelo and Maria should closely follow us up and work in conjunction with us.

As Angie was a born Sicilian mafioso he would be a great asset to our contacts with the Montreal Sicilian bosses. At the very least he would be able to speak the Sicilian dialects.

Firdaussi, once described in Cairo as "a very smart cookie!" was, to me, indispensable. She had saved my bacon (and Angelo's) after our participation in the "Marseilles Massacre" by an astute bit of thinking and, in addition, knew our narcotics and vice business as well as I did.

Maria, Angelo's wife, was a good friend of Firdaussi, but could not be considered to rival her as a clever businesswoman.

However, Maria was one hell of a good belly-dancer, which made up for a lot! We had seen her in action during previous group celebrations. On these occasions our general proclivity was somewhat robust.

In any case Otto Guynemer wanted our wives to go with us to Montreal as social assets, apart from their involvement in the actual negotiations.

Firdaussi and I were told to return to our Corsican base and carry on checking our European business.

Otto and Luigi wanted to plan a foolproof method of eliminating the Corleone menace and spend more time on further contemplation of the Montreal business.

I was told to await further instructions regarding both or either of these matters.

So I returned to Corsica with Firdaussi and spent several days in lazy relaxation. We did not entirely ignore business as we made several 'phone calls to our contact men in Marseilles and Paris to check progress or otherwise.

Our well organized system appeared to be running with its customary smoothness so there were no problems to interfere with our relaxed period.

We felt we were entitled to a little idle time after the concentrated effort we had put into our world shattering murderous affray in Dallas.

Although I must admit I suffered no discomfiture mentally or physically during our escapade due, I guess, to our previous involvement in much more exciting incidents with many more victims to our discredit.

* * * * *

CHAPTER THREE

VISIT TO MONTREAL, CANADA

It was not long before we had word from Luigi to head for Canada and survey the Cosa Nostra scene in Montreal.

Before we went it was necessary to be briefed in detail by Otto Guynemer who could give us introductions to the leading mafiosi in that area.

As Otto had returned to his stately residence at Cottingham Hall in Sussex, England, we had been invited to visit him there to talk in privacy and enjoy the gracious life style of the landed gentry!

We hired an aircraft at Ajaccio airport to take us to Marseilles Marignane where we booked for London. A telephone call to Otto Guynemer disclosing our estimated time of arrival at London Heathrow ensured that someone would be there to pick us up and transport us to Cottingham Hall.

Fred Pierce, Otto's regular chauffeur was there to meet us, holding up his notice spelling DEACON ROY in large letters. Fred had met us at London Heathrow so often that the notice was not really necessary.

However, we were escorted to the big Rolls Royce limousine, our baggage was put in the voluminous trunk and off we sped to Cottingham Hall.

Otto cemented our welcome with an excellent meal, after which we got down to business.

We made ourselves comfortable in the library, fortified with coffee and liqueurs. I made extensive notes of the names and addresses of the Cosa Nostra leaders with whom I was to negotiate.

As usual Firdaussi played her part in the discussion. She asked many valid questions concerning the proposed negotiations, most of which I hadn't thought of!

Thinking of our security she was eager to check on the activities of the local police together with the Canadian federal anti-drug squad.

Was there much violence between rival cartels? Were we to investigate opportunities in other areas?

On this latter subject Otto was clear.

We must inform ourselves on all relevant aspects of the business before we committed ourselves to any group of drug traffickers. We should visit Toronto and Windsor and meet the leading mobsters.

On one point Otto Guynemer was adamant. Under no circumstances were we to cross the border into the United States. As our group had just performed a heinous crime in that country this made sense. The assassination we had engineered would have repercussions for many years and the search for the gunmen by the federal authorities would never cease.

Otto remarked with some vigor, "The longer we stay out of USA the safer we will be. Going there would be like sticking our noses in the lions' den. There are thousands of FBI agents and other federal officers looking for us and most of them will suspect Cosa Nostra involvement."

Otto paused and Firdaussi put her spoke in with, "One great advantage of working through Canada means that we will get our payments in Canada. At present we get our cash in the United States and going there for our money will be added risk."

As usual Firdy was correct!

Luigi sent his underboss Angelo and wife Maria to Cottingham Hall to learn the details from Otto.

It also allowed Angelo and me to plan our moves in Montreal and decide how to indicate our personal relationship to the local mafiosi. Remember Angie was a born Sicilian mafioso and spoke their dialects even though he usually conversed in Chicago American gangster slang as did his boss Don Luigi!

However, his relationship to an obvious English guy speaking a peculiar Limey accent might seem strange to the Montreal mafiosi. We had to overcome this tendency acceptably.

I had worked with Angie on a few major shootings during our cartel's European expansion in addition to our more recent Dallas spectacular. So we knew we could trust each other in most emergencies. On top of which we were not open to bribes from the opposition because, after our huge individual payouts by Otto when we quit Cairo, we were very wealthy citizens!

* * * * *

After a week with Otto Guynemer at Cottingham Hall the four of us left in one of his chauffeur driven Rolls-Royce limousines and headed for London Heathrow airport.

Our flights had been booked in advance so there were no unexpected delays during our trip to Montreal airport.

On landing we were put through the usual brief formalities with Immigration and Customs inspectors before we took a taxi to the hotel recommended by Otto Guynemer. The hotel which had given him good service during his sojourn in Montreal, the Hotel Savoie.

Here we booked a suite for each couple and managed to get dinner even though we had arrived at a late hour.

Next morning, after breakfast, Angelo 'phoned Vincenzo Cotillo to arrange an interview. Vincenzo expected this approach after his earlier discussions with Otto Guynemer.

Vincenzo Cotillo, being the Sicilian mafia boss in Montreal, expected to be treated with due respect. As our high-powered Sicilian cartel under Don Luigi Ferraro felt little respect for anybody we, Angelo, me and our ladies, had to make a special effort to impress Vincenzo Cotillo with our dutiful compliance to Sicilian tradition.

This was actually the keynote of our marketing strategy as our primary aim was to get Vincenzo to ship our massive cargos of heroin and other assorted narcotics through his pipeline to USA, via New York.

We were also assessing the possibilities of breaking into other lucrative local rackets as well as eventually taking over Vincenzo's system either by negotiation, guile or force of arms.

Our group was highly experienced and very adept with the last of these conditions so it might be said that Vincenzo Cotillo was, unknowingly, preparing to take a tiger by the tail.

We hadn't swamped Europe with drugs via Corsica and Naples by being nice to the opposition. Remember the spectacular shoot-outs in Marseilles, Paris and Naples, to name but a few? All craftily engineered by Otto Guynemer and skillfully performed by us, the Good Ol' Boys!

However, during Angelo's 'phone call, Vincenzo Cotillo agreed to meet us without delay at the Pizzeria Portofino on Villeray Street, Montreal.

So we taxied to Villeray Street, leaving Firdaussi and Maria to swan around the better class couturiers in town to check if the standards were acceptable to their refined susceptibilities, remembering their mutual backgrounds!

On entering the Pizzeria Portofino we were welcomed by Vincenzo Cotillo and a hard looking guy named Louis Gratto who we learned was Cotillo's underboss.

Being shown into a back room we soon got down to business. Cotillo opened by stating, "You can talk safely here because Louis owns this pizzeria. Whenever you want to contact me just pass the word to the manager here and I will soon get in touch."

We spent an hour or so discussing general tactics with Cotillo and Gratto, chewing a piece of excellent pizza as we talked.

Agreement was reached on the salient points concerned with shipping and transferring our drug shipments into and out from Montreal. Also the methods of handling our cash payments.

We did not need them to launder our pelf because we had our own comprehensive system which Otto Guynemer and Luigi considered might be used by other cash-burdened drug runners. On paying a useful percentage to us, of course!

No definite commitments were made with these local bosses as we had definite orders from Otto and Luigi to discuss matters with another local big-shot.

This was Nicolo Rizzoli, a Sicilian involved in the narcotics trade and somewhat loosely connected with the Cotillo/Gratto organization. Apart from business Angelo was eager to discover if Nicolo and he were related, each having the same surname.

We had just about finished our discussion with Cotillo and Gratto when who should walk in but Firdaussi and Maria. They had ambled around downtown Montreal and, knowing of our rendezvous with the local boys, decided to come and see what we were up to.

I could see that Cotillo and Gratto were more than impressed with our attractively elegant spouses. After a little small talk we bade our farewells although I sensed we were going to receive some social invitations from Vincenzo Cotillo in the near future. Such are the powers of women!

We taxied back to the Hotel Savoie and enjoyed a good lunch while we discussed our contact with the Cotillo cartel.

Our next move was to talk to Nicolo Rizzoli.

Otto Guynemer had told us how to get in touch with him by 'phone.

He agreed to meet us at yet another pizza parlor, the Pizzeria Romano on Rue Jean-Talon. It seemed to us that every mobster in Quebec used pizza parlors habitually. We discovered the reason later.

We left our hotel early next morning and headed for the Pizzeria Romano. Our spouses undertook their usual hobby of checking out the establishments selling expensive fashions.

Nicolo Rizzoli greeted us affably and escorted us into a private area where we explained our proposals in sufficient detail to get him interested.

We learned that he, with his family, had lived in Montreal for many years. He was also a traditional Sicilian mafioso and tended to mix socially with the numerous similar traditionalists in the area.

He dropped strong hints that, although he was associated business wise with the Cotillo/Gratto mob, he felt that individually he could run the dope racket more efficiently. Angelo and I guessed that this man had secret ambitions. This suited us because we had secret ambitions too!

Our group under Otto Guynemer and Luigi Ferraro had bludgeoned our way into the European drug world by eliminating local mob bosses and replacing them with picked men of our choice. We could do the same in Montreal by neutralizing the Cotillo incumbents and backing Nicolo Rizzoli to act on our behalf. When the opportune time arrived!

We quit Pizzeria Romano in good humor, accompanied by Nicolo who had accepted our invitation to lunch with us, and made our way to Ristorante Palladia where we had booked a table earlier. Nicolo drove us there in his Lincoln.

Firdaussi and Maria were there already knocking back Bloody Mary's (vodka and tomato juice) at ten bucks a time.

This minor indulgence did not affect their affability so we all enjoyed the excellent Italian cuisine. After which we all swigged even more Bloody Mary's with our coffees and even this feat did not affect anyone's affability!

I could sense that our guest, Nicolo Rizzoli, was more than impressed with our friendly demeanor and even with our casual attitude in paying our expensive lunch bill.

By the way, Angelo and Nicolo decided they were distant relatives in the Rizzoli family in Sicily. So distant that neither could specify their relationship in words. This minor default was treated in good humor by both participants.

After further brief discussion Nicolo made his farewells and left but not before assuring us that he would be interested in handling our drug shipments if we so decided.

We felt that things were moving to our advantage in Montreal and mutually proposed that our further visits to the crime bosses in Toronto and Niagara Falls would be cursory in nature.

The accepted suggestion was that we should return to Europe and advise our bosses about our prospects in Montreal. To me these prospects were definitely positive and I intended to convince Otto and Luigi to take action as soon as possible.

I thought we should start trading with Cotillo while encouraging Nicolo Rizzoli to run a lesser share of our drugs to his own advantage. Gradually we would increase Nicolo's share until he felt confident enough to take over Cotillo's business in its entirety.

At that point we would neutralize Cotillo and his cohorts and make Nicolo the big boss in Montreal on the understanding that he was working for us and that our cartel was actually the big boss!

This system had made us the top brass in Europe and I considered it should work equally to our advantage in Canada.

An unexpected incident occurred before we left Montreal. Cotillo's underboss, Louis Gratto was accidentally killed by a fire in his pizzeria. We gave the appropriate condolences but did not loiter and left for Europe without delay.

Coincidentally, as we were on the point of leaving, a message was received from Luigi telling us to return direct to his fief in Sicily where he and Otto Guynemer had information for us.

CHAPTER FOUR

THE CORLEONE PROBLEM

As we guessed the expected information from Otto and Don Luigi concerned the extirpation of Pacelli and the leading members of the Corleone family.

The village of Corleone was over one hundred miles from Luigi's working area so I guessed it would have to be a long-distance job, a fact which added to the obvious dangers involved when facing the experienced assassins in the Corleone family.

I wondered what kind of plan Otto and Luigi had formulated. After all our cartel contained some very experienced killers too. An interesting situation was developing!

* * * * *

The murder plan was influenced by a startling incident in Palermo, the capital town of Sicily, in 1963. This was the killing of seven carabinieri in a mafia organized car-bomb explosion.

This drastic deed caused a violent reaction from the Italian government which flooded Sicily with large numbers of carabinieri supported by numerous squads of soldiers. They were under the control of a very tough senior officer who was determined to wreck the criminal mafia system. To this end he arrested so many mafia leaders that the gaols in Sicily were over filled. The carabinieri are, of course, Italian paramilitary police.

By luck, bribery and location in the south-eastern area of the island, Don Luigi's manor was relatively unaffected by the official disruptive efforts which were chiefly concentrated centrally and in the west areas where the majority mafia families were situated.

Otto Guynemer and Don Luigi Ferraro had, in their customary cold-blooded manner, calculated that it would be essential to decimate the Corleone family in their own domain, some hundred miles to the west.

This would mean transporting the chosen gunmen there by the most suitable method. The most suitable method would have to afford a measure of anonymity to the perpetrators of the mass killing in order to preclude the possibility that Don Luigi Ferraro’s family could be definitely identified as responsible.

Luigi was aware that his outfit would be suspect but he wanted to reduce the chance of definite recognition by hostile witnesses.

So approaching the target by rail or air were, after due consideration, both eliminated as unsuitable methods of transport.

This left travel by road to be discussed and at this stage of planning Otto Guynemer and Luigi had strong memories of a previous occasion when their Cairo syndicate had smuggled illicit firearms into Palestine using a military truck manned by a pseudo-military crew.*

* * * * *

Angelo and I had been sitting around a table sipping our glasses of Sicilian red wine as we listened to Otto and Luigi formulating their scheme for the assassination of the leading Corleone mafiosi.

Luigi addressed me with, " You will remember, Deac, when you, Abdul and Igor took that load of choppers to Palestine in a military truck which we managed to buy second-hand?"

I responded, "I sure do, Luigi," and added with a grin, "And I well remember the gunfight with the phony policemen which put me in temporary shock!"

Both Luigi and Otto echoed my grin as Luigi countered my remark with, "I guess you’ve learned a bit since those days, Deac."

Angelo caught my eye and added with smiling emphasis, "He most certainly has!"

* See "The Cairo Connection", Page 36

Otto continued the discourse, surveying Angie and me with a speculative gaze, " Neither of you will be surprised to hear, building on past experience, that we have obtained a local military truck which will suit our purpose absolutely."

He paused to sip his wine, glanced at Luigi with a knowing smile and continued, "Neither will you be surprised to know that Luigi insists on leading this expedition as he considers a personal threat should be wiped out personally!"

Otto went on, "Of course you will accompany Luigi, both of you and with you in the truck will be four trusted "soldiers" from Luigi's mafia family. The way you three leaders handled the Dallas affair should add to your confidence in the eventual success of this Corleone business."

He stopped his monologue while he lit up one of his aromatic Cuban cheroots and inhaled with leisurely satisfaction.

We waited, quietly eager to learn more.

Then Otto carried on while Luigi nodded occasional assent to the main details. He started, " We have learned that Don Pacelli, his underboss, his consigliere and probably about six of his senior capodecina have been invited to a grand fiesta, together with their women, at Marineo. The invite has come from the Don of a local family which is known to be closely cooperative with the Corleone mob due to close proximity and fear of its tyrannical neighbors. In other words the Marineo outfit are eager to gain the further favor of Pacelli."

Luigi took over the spiel at this stage.

Stubbing out the last of his seemingly endless Luckies he proceeded, "I have ordered a couple of my young soldiers, innocently riding motor cycles as if on vacation, to spend a few days in the Marineo area checking on access, the fiesta site, the frequency of military and carabinieri trucks and men around the location and other relevant factors. After receiving and considering their reports," Luigi paused and glanced at Otto, "We have decided to make a frontal attack on our targets shortly after their reception as guests.

We propose to enter the site in our military uniforms, weapons in hand, as if we are on a routine inspection. You will be aware that police and military inspections are common and expected after that stupid massacre of carabinieri in Palermo."

Luigi halted his details and lit another Luckie.

"Any questions?" he asked.

"How the hell am I going to know the Corleone individuals?" I asked abruptly, "Surely they will be mixed up with the local mob who invited them to the fiesta."

"No worry, Deac," Luigi replied, "I'll be the first to open fire and my target will be Bernardo Pacelli. I want the rest of you guys to mow down every man in his close vicinity. For sure the majority will be Corleone boys as Pacelli demands close support and protection from his cohorts under all circumstances, even at a so-called "friendly" fiesta. To Pacelli, as well he knows, very few people are truly friendly.

If we knock off one or two of the local Marieno jerks put it down to accidental death!" Quite a wag, our Luigi!

"So as soon as I blast Pacelli open fire goddamned pronto on your targets because every one of them will carry a gun and won't be slow to draw it.

I want this hit to be over in seconds and not develop into a gunfight with casualties on our side." A short pause.

"D'ya get that, Deac?" Luigi finished.

"Sure, I get it, Luigi." I responded, "And what about the women who will certainly be closely involved with our targets?"

Luigi made his reply with his usual cold-blooded confidence, "The dames will have to take their chance, if some of them stop a few of our slugs then so-be-it. It's the men we are after, if they are rubbed out then anything else is acceptable."

Angelo put in his query, "O.K. so we knock off the chief members of the opposition, or so we hope, what happens as we rapidly retreat if a couple or more triggermen are alive and kicking and open fire on our backs?"

"No problem, Angie," Luigi answered," I have ordered two of my family "soldiers" to hold their fire while we do the real shooting and to concentrate on guarding our backs as we beat it."

Luigi gulped his wine, stubbed his cigarette and lit up another from his case.

Otto took over with, "And as you leave the arena you will not be jumping in our military truck to make your getaway. The truck will be cached a couple of kilometers away on the road back. If we have it waiting for you outside the killing zone it will be recognizable and some respectable citizen may blab about it to the law.

A civilian pick-up truck will be waiting and will speed you along the road to our military wagon which will bring you home.

The pick-up truck will be driven far away into a remote region and dropped into a lake, to vanish forever."

"So when is the big day?" I queried.

Otto started to answer but withdrew as Luigi interjected, " It should be a week from now but I gotta re-check for sure. We don't wanna turn up and discover there ain't no goddamned fiesta!"

We chuckled as we agreed with this manifest remark.

Angie was next with, "What are we using to do the shooting, Luigi?"

Otto broke in with a smile, "You may remember, Angelo, that you are a director of our Pharos International company as we all are. You know our firm is authorized to deal in firearms and munitions officially so you won't be surprised to hear that we have a dozen Uzi sub-machine guns stashed away with a plentiful supply of 9 mm. shells ready for use as and when required."

That little monologue satisfied Angelo just as it satisfied me. We all had recollections of a very effective performance with the Uzi in Naples when we gave the comeuppance to the then boss of the Camorra plus several of his henchmen.

Luigi finished our initial meeting by informing us, "I have picked the men who are accompanying us on this caper; two reliable "soldiers", both members of my family; the senior capodecina, another family member; my consigliere, Enrico Campagna, who, as you all know, was my right hand man in our Resistance movement against the Nazis in WW2."

Angie and I grunted and nodded our approval of this strong addition to our fighting strength.

Luigi added, "There will be a couple more reliable "soldiers" to drive our truck and the pick-up wagon."

He went on, "I intend to run a couple rehearsals of our tactics in the next couple of days to make sure we all know what the hell we are involved in and how to act in military uniforms. Otto will keep an experienced eye on our procedures and give any needed advice."

With that statement the meeting closed.

CHAPTER FIVE

THE MARIENO MASSACRE

We performed our practice sessions without undue trouble. Our gang mounted and dismounted to and from our military truck fully clothed in our uniforms and carrying our Uzi guns and ammo.

We did the same procedure with the pick-up vehicle and Otto made us carry out this feat in a hurry as we needed a rapid getaway after the hoped for slaughter of the Corleone mob.

All concerned were made to shoot their now personal Uzi sub-machine guns at ingeniously placed man-size targets, arranged to be as much like the expected murder zone as possible.

This exercise was timed and the total number of hits counted carefully because we were all shooting together as we would be on the killing day.

We were limited to two Uzi magazines each so, under Luigi's surveillance, we had to practice a fast magazine change over and over again.

To facilitate this manoever we clamped our two magazines together in the accepted military fashion so that on removing the finished magazine from the gun and reversing it the new full magazine was in the correct position for inserting into the gun.

A neckerchief was supplied to each of us which we were instructed to wear around our necks under our uniforms. These could be pulled up to cover our faces from our eyes down as we entered the killing area and would give us a good measure of anonymity.

This technique, in fact, was quite usual during operations by the carabinieri when they were hunting wanted mafiosi after the ruthless massacre of their comrades in Palermo.

One problem was ensuring Bernardo Pacelli was at the fiesta before we arrived to kill him!

Otto and Luigi had solved this little difficulty.

One of Luigi's motor cycle boys would see the Pacelli gang arrive, then he would tear along the road to meet our truck and pass on the good news. We would then proceed on our mission.

* * * * *

Came the day when we mounted the military truck with our weapons and full uniforms.

Luigi sat in the cab with the driver and we set off on our somewhat tedious trip at 9 am.

After a hearty breakfast, enjoyed by all, as we felt it would be inconvenient to stop for lunch at Marieno after murdering the opposition!

We cruised along the main route for three hours and halted at a secluded spot under the trees on a side road; an area ten miles from the fiesta site.

There we sat and waited for at least thirty minutes, puffing our cigarettes and wondering where the hell our motor-cycle messenger had got to.

Naturally he had been previously instructed where we would be so he had no difficulty in contacting us.

When he arrived, obviously excited, he almost fell off his bike as he skidded to a halt.

"They're there, a dozen of them including four ladies," he hurriedly babbled to Luigi, his Don. And continued, " I left as soon as they entered the fiesta garden and came here as fast as I could."

My basic Italian helped me understand his local Sicilian dialect.

Luigi queried, also in dialect, "Are you certain Don Pacelli was one of them?"

"Oh, yes Sir," answered the lad, "I recognized him immediately."

"You're a good soldier," replied Luigi. A compliment from his Don which brought a beam of delight to the young man's face.

"Let's go," ordered the Don, "We'll hit them as they are enjoying the traditional welcoming buffet if we get a move on!"

Luigi always favored the grimmer sort of wisecrack!

Our driver drove the truck to the fiesta site at high speed. It took about fifteen minutes.

On arrival we rapidly de-bussed and, with Luigi in the lead, entered the garden in a compact group. Angelo and I kept close to our boss, Angie on his left with me on his right hand side.

We three leaders were more than familiar with calculated assassinations!

There was a large marquee set up in the garden to allow comfort to the invitees by offering shaded shelter from the intrusively bright sun.

As we strode towards the marquee entrance, pulling up our neckerchiefs over our faces, we saw two guys standing outside, armed with shotguns, obviously guards but not noticeably alert to the danger approaching.

In fact they appeared to be enjoying the sound of sweet music emanating from the marquee!

However they did notice the pseudo-military squad approaching and one made cautious remonstrance, in dialect, saying there was no need for police inspection at a respectable fiesta.

Luigi responded in military fashion by barking, also in dialect, "Shut up, you insolent bastard or you'll be arrested!"

So the guy shut up as politely requested!

Our group entered the marquee and rapidly assessed the situation.

There was Pacelli, standing near the buffet table, with a cigarette in one hand and a glass of red wine in the other. Three cronies were talking with him and partaking of the red wine in their turns.

Luigi opened fire immediately at less than five yards range and Pacelli was dead before he was aware of the imminent danger.

He must have noticed our entry but about two seconds later a dozen 9 mm. slugs from Luigi's Uzi had torn his body apart.

Me and Angelo opened fire simultaneously a fraction of a second after Luigi. We blew Pacelli's three henchmen away and coincidentally built a gruesome heap of four twitching cadavers, including their boss Pacelli.

Luigi's capodecina and his consigliere, Enrico Campagna, picked a few other startled Corleone family members as their targets. The roar of gunfire was incredible in that far from solid marquee.

There were terrified screams from the women when they realized that Doomsday had arrived for many of their relatives.

Five of us were doing the executions, the two young "soldiers" had been instructed to guard our backs as we retreated.

The initial gunfire petered out as our first batch of ammo. was shot away. We rapidly changed magazines and looked for more targets.

The capodecina and Enrico Campagna noticed a couple of panic stricken heroes groveling under the big buffet table. Short bursts from their Uzi guns ensured these gentlemen would stay there for a bit longer than they expected.

I was almost the last of our guys to shoot.

As I edged along the table I saw a lady furtively draw a pistol from her handbag and hand it to her male companion.

He, brave man, started to raise it in our direction.

I squeezed the trigger and my Uzi sent the last dozen of my bullets into his head and body. His bloody, grimacing face stared at me through his one remaining eye as he mouthed silent words before he dropped grotesquely to the floor.

His lady friend picked up his dropped revolver with the obvious intention of using it but I had fired all the slugs in my Uzi so I was unable to shoot her. I was reaching for my pistol when Angie solved the problem with a short burst from his Uzi.

This courageous lady screamed in sudden agony as Angie's bullets ripped into her slender body causing her to collapse on top of her dead boy friend, her summer dress sodden with the blood gushing from her multiple wounds.

At this stage Luigi shouted the order to quit.

We made for the exit, pistols in hand as our Uzi magazines were empty.

The two guards, who I am sure thought we were genuine paramilitary personnel, made a half-hearted attempt at resistance. Half-hearted because of the recent prolonged gunfire in the marquee which indicated we were not to be toyed with!

Unfortunately for them our two young "soldiers" noticed the tentative movement of the guards' shotguns in our direction and immediately riddled them with long bursts from their Uzi guns.

This rapid reaction ensured there was no interruption in our getaway.

I considered the young "soldiers" were eager to be involved in the action and were elated that the two now defunct guards had made a hesitant move which could have been interpreted as threatening.

We boarded our pick-up truck without undue haste and were driven back to our military wagon.

Luigi instructed us to leave our used Uzi guns and magazines in the pick-up truck and informed the driver the arms were to stay there when he ran the vehicle over the high cliff from where it would drop into the lake. A very deep lake!

To ensure this was done the capodecina departed in the pick-up to supervise the action was completed.

Luigi had always insisted, to my knowledge, that all firearms used in a shooting should be dropped in the ocean or otherwise permanently disposed of as soon as possible.

As he said, "There's some smart-assed forensic cops who can get a lot of info. from a used firearm. Don't help 'em to hang you!"

So we had invariably followed his professional advice.

We returned to Luigi's manor without problem. Enrico Campagna and the young "soldiers" were sent on their way, exulting in the thanks of their Don for a job well done, well aware they would be adequately rewarded for their efforts.

There was no need to tell the participants in the slaughter to keep their mouths shut as they were all mafiosi born and bred (except me!) and knew the stringent penalties for non-compliance.

As for me, I had worked with the Cosa Nostra very closely and had learned about the penalties at an early stage in my career!

Luigi, Angelo and I were welcomed home with relief by our loving wives and Otto Guynemer.

We tore ourselves away from our ladies' embraces, cleaned up and sat down to a superb meal.

"A late lunch!" some wag remarked.

Of course there were many questions about our recent escapade but we did not disclose the gruesome details in front of the women. Just the generalities!

The details would be pondered on in private with Otto Guynemer when we would consider the possible developments ensuing after our bloody elimination of the Corleone threat.

* * * * *

Otto Guynemer was highly pleased that the tactics he had plotted with Luigi for our latest assassination had worked out successfully.

In my time with the Cosa Nostra every premeditated murderous affray undertaken by our group had been planned in detail by Otto with the close cooperation of Luigi, the old professional, who had learned his business in the Chicago of Al Capone's day.

We had put Bernardo Pacelli and at least nine other of his myrmidons out of business permanently at the Marieno fiesta so we calculated there would be a big brou-ha-ha from the other mafia families and, above all, the law.

Our main concern was if someone unseen by us had witnessed our antics and could prove we were Don Luigi Ferraro's family.

This was highly unlikely after the precautions we had taken. In effect our murderous effort was completed in less than two minutes.

The suddenness of our attack and the associated shock effect on those people left alive were not conducive to a calm assessment of the identities of the shooters.

The chief aim of all those in the target zone, men and women, was to get out of the field of fire.

This general tendency included the automatic impulse to crouch, shield the head and eyes. A disposition which would render it almost impossible to recognise the attackers.

However, as time progressed, we discovered that the consensus of opinion among the Cosa Nostra families and their associates was that the massacre had indeed been committed by a regular squad of the paramilitary police intent on revenge for the slaying of their comrades in the Palermo shooting.

This false conjecture was, of course, very pleasing to our

bunch of hoodlums. We had half-expected some violent form of retaliation by the remaining members of the Corleone mob. Now everybody seemed to blame the carabinieri for the dirty deed!

Luigi, as usual, could not refrain from sarcastic comment, " As our uniforms were so doggone effective it may pay some of us to wear them permanent. It sure would improve some guy's looks!"

My wife Ferdaussi added, "Some looks would be improved if you all kept the neckerchiefs over your faces!"

A smart cookie was Ferdaussi, and had been, more than once in the past, a lot smarter than the rest of us.

These little bursts of jocularity helped us relax after the tension involved in our escapade at the fiesta.

Thinking back I never looked upon it as a successful fiesta for the invitees!

The military and police seemed to undertake a mere cursory investigation into the Marieno shooting even though it was comparatively large scale.

As they had been sent to Sicily in their thousands by the Italian government with express instructions to eradicate the mafia, their Commanding General, a hard-bitten senior officer, probably considered the killings to be a help rather than a hindrance.

So we had no problems with the law.

* * * * *

CHAPTER SIX

THE CANADIAN CONNECTION

After a couple days discussion concerning our numerous business ventures Firdaussi and I received our marching orders.

Luigi told us to return to our home in Corsica, check on our appointed racket bosses in Marseilles and Paris to ensure the European drug distribution was proceeding as ordered and wait for further instructions.

The further instructions would be concerned with again visiting Montreal, Canada, to transfer our drug shipments to Vincenzo Cotillo, the Cosa Nostra chief in that city.

Otto Guynemer, when the time came, would arrive in Montreal to oversee negotiations with Cotillo and add the weight of vast experience to our discussions.

Angelo and wife Maria would also be included in our team as we had secret plans connected with Nicolo Rizzoli who happened to be a far distant relative of Angie. Nicolo was another prominent Cosa Nostra drug trafficker based in Canada.

* * * * *

On arrival in Montreal Firdaussi and I headed for the Savoie Hotel as we had done on our previous visit. We booked a suite and ordered dinner.

Angelo and Maria turned up just after us. We rarely traveled in a group as we had no wish to be noticed when proceeding on business.

However, the four of us had dinner together and took the opportunity to plan our next moves. Otto Guynemer would probably join us the next day so we prepared ourselves for an early visit to Vincenzo Cotillo.

I proposed we should contact Cotillo as soon as possible to

let him know we were in Montreal. This would warn him that negotiations were imminent and so allow him to get ready to make a suitable deal.

As expected Otto Guynemer booked in at the Savoie Hotel next morning and, after a short discussion with us, 'phoned Vincenzo Cotillo and arranged a meeting.

I was rather surprised to learn from Otto that Cotillo had suggested he should come to the Savoie Hotel with his new underboss for the conference. Surprised because our previous meetings had taken place in various pizza parlours around Montreal. Privately owned by Cosa Nostra members, of course, to afford privacy.

However, on hearing Cotillo's proposal, Otto invited him and his henchman to have lunch with our group at the hotel, adding we would pursue our negotiations afterwards in a private room.

Cotillo and his cohort soon appeared and were very affable in their approach to us. Especially, I noted, to our shapely, expensively dressed wives, Firdaussi and Maria!

We had all met Vincenzo during our previous visit to Montreal so he introduced us to his underboss, Paolo Velio.

Velio was a big, fat guy, dressed decently and apparently friendly although, from his habitually sour-puss mien, I guessed he could be rather belligerent when the occasion arose.

I discovered later that Velio was not Sicilian mafia. His family originated in Calabria, Southern Italy and was basically *'ndrangheta*. A term which can be roughly translated as Calabrian mafia.

This difference in origin tended to raise certain difficulties among the criminal elements in Montreal at a later date.

Nevertheless, we all enjoyed a delectable meal and, after our coffee and brandies, politely shooed off our glamorous female accomplices in crime to spend our pelf with upscale couturiers.

Then the five men involved retired to the pre-booked private conference room for the pending negotiations.

The language used was English although our close colleague Angelo, a born and bred Sicilian mafioso, interposed in local dialect when required.

Otto, Angie and I were not in suppliant mood during our long conversation. We controlled vast quantities of drugs and, in addition, were running much into the United States of America successfully. Our huge money laundering operation would probably have made Cotillo and his mob appear to be small fry.

On top of which, considering Don Luigi's facilities in Sicily, we could call on experienced hit-men to solve any problems requiring a violent conclusion.

So, our attitude during the negotiations was far removed from humble compliance with local demands.

I felt we were doing the local jerks a favor!

Apart from such inner feelings the negotiations proceeded fairly smoothly.

Vincenzo Cotillo seemed quite keen to work with our cartel and I supposed that he was influenced by the fact that Otto Guynemer had been introduced to him in the first instance by Joe Bonnano, boss of the powerful New York Cosa Nostra family.

With that kind of reference we should be worth cooperating with. On the other hand Paolo Velio found it hard to agree with the most basic of our suggestions.

His main intention appeared to be to impress us with the great power he and Cotillo wielded over the Canadian drug scene. I surmised that Cotillo gave his supposed underboss too much scope in organizing their business.

Paolo Velio even lost his temper at one stage, much to Cotillo's discomfiture and to our secret amusement.

The fat man asked us abruptly where we were smuggling our current shipments of dope across the US border.

"Where you pushing your heroin over the line to the States?" he queried, glaring at us, sour faced as usual

I replied concisely with an intentional broad smile, " Firstly, Paolo, we're pushing more than heroin and secondly we never tell our routes to strangers as we have learned not to trust many of them."

Paolo nearly blew up! His face turned scarlet and he leaned across the table aggressively in such a manner that I expected him to strike me.

"So you don't trust me, eh?" he yelled, "Let me tell you guys that you'll get nowhere in Quebec without our permission, so remember who the hell you're talking to!"

Vincenzo Cotillo succeeded in calming down his obnoxious cohort but I was aware that from then on I was not a favorite of Paolo Velio.

It was a certainty that the fat man wanted everybody in the rackets to be scared of him.

I was his first mistake!

In spite of this minor altercation business was completed satisfactorily. Cotillo and Guynemer, the two bosses, agreed on the important points with some input from Angelo and I. Paolo Velio added little to the business after our clash, sitting glowering at nothing and chain smoking without cease.

It was suggested that I should check and supervise our first shipment of narcotics through the docks. This included preparing substantial illicit regular payments to sundry crooked officials and dock workers.

Both Angelo and I would be involved in ensuring that Cotillo's group passed the shipments on to the Sicilian Cosa Nostra element of the New York Bonnano crime family. There was no question, obviously, of either of us visiting the United States after our Dallas venture.

Most important was the requirement of getting payment for our goods. This would certainly be in US dollars cash, usually in a bulky wad, requiring processing by our extensive world-wide money laundering facility.

The meeting broke up with general satisfaction all round although I noticed, with some amusement, that the temporarily affable Paolo avoided shaking hands with me when he and his boss left us.

Cotillo was quite pleased with the progress we had made and invited us, and our ladies, to dinner at his home the following evening.

We accepted gratefully as Cotillo remarked that certain of his colleagues would be present, this fact giving us the opportunity to meet the principal people involved in the local rackets, drug and otherwise.

* * * * *

The rest of the day and most of the next day were spent in intense discussion by the three of us plus Firdaussi and Maria.

The ladies, especially Firdy my wife, knew as much about our rackets as I did and invariably added to our discourse some important words of wisdom concerning salient points which the men had probably forgotten or ignored. Clever gals indeed!

We had to gradually unwind our current system whereby our own cargo vessel proceeded to St. John, New Brunswick from Europe and smuggled our shipments of dope over the Canada/USA border into the state of Maine for further distribution throughout the United States.

This was an intensively expensive and complicated procedure which could not be finalized overnight.

In the long run our vessel with our contraband cargo would sail direct to the St Lawrence seaway and Montreal, no problem, but in the meanwhile it would have to call at both ports. This included, among other things, the payment of extensive bribes to sundry officials and dock workers at both New Brunswick and Montreal.

We would have to work fast and it would be necessary for Angelo and me both to reside in Canada for some considerable time.

Otto would be returning to Europe to discuss details with Luigi and ensure that our venture in Canada would not impair our huge European organization.

To add to our problems Otto insisted that we should open a branch of our very legal commercial company in Toronto. The leading members of our cartel had all, including Firdaussi, been appointed directors of Pharos International. This company dealt in anything which made a profit, duly licensed and officially accepted to the degree that government contracts were common.

This business was the brain-child of Otto Guynemer as was the North Delta Trading Corporation during our mob's Cairo, Egypt, period. Otto was the president and overall controller of Pharos International, a London registered outfit.

The advantage of opening Pharos International in Toronto was the legitimate cover it would give to me and Angelo and any other of our cartel who were working in Canada. Without this cover some smart-assed cop would inevitably ponder on what we were doing during our prolonged visits to Canada, especially if we were observed with local crime bosses.

As senior executives of an important international company we would probably pass muster by inquisitive officials.

Before Otto Guynemer returned to Europe he intended to come with the rest of us to Vincenzo Cotillo's dinner date.

Cotillo lived in upmarket style in Woodbridge, not a great distance from our hotel.

All five of us traveled there by taxi at the appointed hour and discovered a small fleet of expensive automobiles parked in Cotillo's driveway and nearby. It was obviously intended to be a substantial dinner party. I felt that the main purpose of our invitation was to be introduced to our host's close cronies.

And so it was. Besides Vincenzo Cotillo, supported by sour-faced Paolo Velio, there were another five couples, all well dressed, the men in tuxedos with their fashionably dressed womenfolk assessing our glamorous Firdaussi and Maria with more than passing interest. I guessed they were mentally appraising our gals' top-of-the market European apparel and wishing they themselves had the figures to wear something similar!

We were welcomed by the group in affable fashion while being introduced to all and sundry.

I even suffered a reluctant handshake from my recent antagonist Paolo Velio!

The best part of half-hour was spent in general chatter, mostly in English when Otto Guynemer, Firdaussi and I were included in conversations. However, it must be remembered that everybody else at the dinner party spoke Italian or some Sicilian dialect in addition to English, including Angelo and Maria, so there was a constant buzz of talk in these tongues as we sipped our aperitifs.

Eventually we sat down to dinner, nineteen of us, at a large, tastefully dressed table, our group of five being seated adjacent to Cotillo and wife as we were considered guests of honor.

I must say we were treated with great hospitality during our visit and it was apparent that Otto Guynemer attracted impressive deference from the men, all Cosa Nostra affiliates.

They were doubtless aware he had been introduced to the Montreal mob by none other than New York Cosa Nostra boss Joe Bonnano, virtual controller of the Montreal Sicilian element.

Hence the respect.

I looked around the table and, rather derisively, considered that Otto was probably the wealthiest guy present; remembering his vast payoffs, legal and illegal, during his Cairo period; his splendid country estate Cottingham Hall in Sussex, England; his presidency of the flourishing Pharos International Corporation plus his current take from our huge European/American drug and vice rackets, led me to assume that he could buy and sell most guys around.

I was pleased to see our previous acquaintance Nicolo Rizzoli was at the table.

As mentioned before I was mentally engineering an ingenious plot to incorporate Nicolo in our future depredations in Canada.

On our side and terms, of course!

That this would surely entail the violent elimination of most of the other local men at the dinner table troubled my conscience not a whit.

I had long since established my impenitent attitude to the murderous affrays involved in our global crime build-up and gloried in the rewards accrued by these methods. In this I was at one with my accomplices in the Luigi Ferraro Cosa Nostra family.

We had not come to Canada to perpetually hand our drug shipments to Vincenzo Cotillo for dispatch to the United States. Our intention was to take over and control the Canadian drug and vice rackets as we had done in Europe.

To spiritually assist us in this endeavor we had a formidable series of assassinations to our joint discredit!

Furthermore we would have no hesitation in adding chosen victims to the list when our business program necessitated such action.

The excellent repast provided by Vincenzo Cotillo proceeded with much congeniality all round. Even fat man Paolo Velio muttered a few agreeable words to me, the guy who had more or less threatened me only yesterday! This jerk seemed to have two faces, one affable and generous, the other downright nasty and aggressive.

Otto Guynemer had been asked by Cotillo to address the diners briefly during the coffee and liqueurs period. He performed this, to Otto, small chore with ease and some caution.

Cautious was Otto because he never did believe in shooting his mouth off to comparative strangers. Especially when serious business was concerned.

After Otto had concluded his impressive monologue, chiefly generalities subtly disguised as important statements, there was spontaneous applause from the audience which convinced our little group that Otto had done it yet again. He had steered Don Luigi Ferraro's cartel into eventual domination of the local scene.

We left the table and, after half-hour of friendly discussion with our new acquaintances, the party broke up with Vincenzo Cotillo and his wife escorting us to the door.

I had made a point of talking to Nicolo Rizzoli, suggesting that I would like him to have another meeting with us in the near future. He agreed and, with his wife, unexpectedly volunteered to drive our group of five back to the Savoie Hotel.

This offer saved us calling a taxi so, with much jollity, we crushed into his Lincoln sedan with Firdaussi and Maria sitting on their respective spouses knees, which was not unpleasant!

As this maneuver progressed I noticed Paolo Velio watching us, sour faced, and noting our familiarity with Nicolo Rizzoli. I suspected he was not over-fond of Nicolo.

On arrival at the Savoie we invited Nicolo and spouse in for even more convivial drinks, an offer which they accepted eagerly.

I sensed they were both keen to get on closer relations with our group and I took advantage of this supposition by asking Nicolo quietly, point blank, "What is your personal opinion of Paolo Velio, Nicolo?"

Nicolo looked around with some caution before responding, just as quietly, "He's a bloated big-mouthed bastard who thinks he knows it all and, although he's underboss to Vincenzo Cotillo, is personally convinced that he's the big boss who controls the Quebec and Ontario rackets." Nicolo paused briefly to light a cigarette and offer me one.

He continued, "When Cotillo's previous underboss died I think he bungled badly by making Paolo Velio his number two man. Since Velio shot and killed a man in Toronto, admitted his guilt to the law and was let off on a self -defence plea, he thinks everybody fears him and acts aggressively to get his own way."

I butted in here with, " A fact I am well aware of, Nicolo, as I suffered under his tactless approach after I clashed with him a couple of days ago."

Nicolo nodded his understanding of my interjection and

pursued his discourse, "You know he is Calabrian, Deacon, and my Sicilian friends locally are getting more and more impatient with his methods and attitudes."

Nicolo stopped and looked around at our little group because Otto and Angelo had listened closely to our conversation. He sipped his drink, inhaled deeply, and added a valid question, "Now you all know my opinion, will you tell me yours?"

Otto responded without hesitation, "Your opinion exactly reflects our feelings on the subject, Nicolo, but we will keep our sentiments confidential until the time comes to make our own arrangements, agreed?" Otto finalized with, "And that time will not be too long delayed, Nicolo."

Nicolo looked faintly relieved as he assented to Otto's question, being now certain that our cartel intended to do our own thing in spite of Cotillo and Velio's apparent dominance locally.

Meanwhile our ladies, Firdaussi and Maria, had been indulging in a good old gossip with Nicolo's wife, Giuseppa. As usual our girls had no trouble winning their new acquaintance over and the air was full of responsive jollity and bursts of feminine laughter!

This formed a good cover for the more serious discussion between the menfolk.

Nicolo and Giuseppa left for home after another drink or two but not before inviting us all to a meal at their residence in the near future at some mutually acceptable date.

* * * * *

CHAPTER SEVEN

TROUBLE AHEAD

Otto Guynemer decided to return to Sicily for discussion with Luigi about the latest developments with Vincenzo Cotillo, the reigning Cosa Nostra boss in Montreal. Not forgetting our impressions of Cotillo's underboss Paolo Velio, impressions which tended to be more than a little unfavorable.

Otto had left Angelo and me, together with Firdaussi and Maria, with a lot of organizational work to get on with promptly.

Our two bosses in Europe intended to undertake changing our cartel owned cargo vessel's route to North America thus saving us guys a tedious chore which it would be difficult to undertake from Montreal. Instead of heading for Saint John, New Brunswick our load of dope would be shipped in future direct to Montreal docks where Cotillo's group would be responsible for unloading the narcotics and evading inspection by the Customs authority.

Otto had left me with the task of setting up a Canadian branch office of our legal UK company Pharos International Corporation. He had previously suggested this office should be in Toronto but told me to set it up in Montreal if I considered this the most convenient situation. Even though Pharos would be trading normally the main purpose of the firm would be to give us a legal cover for our continued presence in Canada.

There was also the problem of finding decent accommodation for our little gang. We did not want apartments where prying eyes could note our comings and goings. So we hunted around for private houses out of the direct vision of neighbors.

Or rather our two wives hunted around for suitable residences as they were well aware of the essential requirements. Knowing their expensive tastes Angelo and I knew in advance that they would choose considerably up-market locations!

How right we were! We finished up with quite luxurious dwellings, one for each couple with all the amenities. By good luck or, perhaps, good judgment they were about a quarter mile apart, each on a large well treed private lot.

We inspected these buildings, accompanied by the happy realtor, paid for them promptly and left most of the furnishing requirements to our wives.

They, as usual, spent our money lavishly and wisely. So we finished up with really up-market digs.

Angie and I swanned around Montreal looking for transport. We each bought a Cadillac sedan and I added to my garage with a Buick convertible. This latter was for use by all of us as required.

Of course, all the automobiles we had purchased could be used at will by Luigi and Otto Guynemer when they visited Canada.

In fact, the houses and the cars were, in effect, business assets to be used freely by our cartel members when necessary.

Our domestic arrangements were also comfortably expensive. As neither wife was addicted to working in the kitchen on culinary matters we usually had a light breakfast and ate most other meals in carefully chosen restaurants.

On those occasions when we decided to invite guests to dinner, or whatever, we employed a caterer with all the trimmings.

As soon as we had settled in our new abodes I concentrated on finding a suitable office for installing our strictly legal company, Pharos International Corporation. To perform this function satisfactorily it was necessary to keep in constant touch with Otto Guynemer.

Otto, of course, had set up Pharos and kept hands on control of the head office in London, UK. Although all the leading Sicilian cartel members (and their wives!) were ostensibly company directors and shareholders, Otto Guynemer was the actual company president and had built the firm's business up to international level with important contracts from many sources including various government departments in numerous countries.

Otto told me to pick a few likely sites for the new office and wait for him and Luigi to visit us shortly, at which time we could make a group decision. Or, at least I felt, Otto would make it look like a group decision!

Luigi was keen to personally check the difficult situation developing between our acquaintance Nicolo Rizzoli and his *bete noire* Paolo Velio. I was convinced this difficulty could be exploited to our advantage, as did Luigi.

He wished to converse more with the people involved and judge just how far we could go without jeopardizing our own very large drug trafficking business with Canada and USA.

* * * * *

Luigi and his wife Tania arrived together with Otto, disembarking at Montreal Airport.

Angie and I, accompanied by Maria and Firdaussi respectively, picked them up in our brand-new Cadillacs and transported them to our brand-new homesteads.

It was decided (by the bosses!) that Luigi and Tania would bunk at our place. There was more than enough room and Otto would stay with Angelo.

As both our domiciles could be considered well on their way to being luxurious the newcomers would not be suffering to any degree. In addition, the fact that the houses were not far apart made communication between us simple.

Our ladies were overjoyed at all being together again and were soon planning excursions around Montreal, using our Buick convertible, to show Tania the sights and , no doubt, to spend a lot of money while doing so!

As stated before our highly respectable, highly attractive and highly up-market spouses were all ex-prostitutes who joined their highly criminal mates during our highly lucrative sojourn in Cairo, Egypt.

Hence their communal conviviality!

Once our bosses had settled in comfortably we sallied forth for a decent dinner at the Hotel Metropolitan restaurant which had been recommended to Firdaussi by a couturier who had custom-made some dresses for her.

During the excellent meal it was suggested by Otto Guynemer that we should use the next day to finalize the choice of site for our local Pharos International Corporation branch.

This was agreed. Luigi followed by stating that he wanted us to invite Nicolo Rizzoli to dinner as he wished to feed him with a few hints about our future intentions and judge if his reactions were suitable enough to include him in our proposed scheme to oust Vincenzo Cotillo from his position as current crime boss in the Montreal/Toronto area.

I contacted Nicolo Rizzoli promptly and he accepted our invitation to dinner just as promptly the date being fixed for the day after tomorrow.

We had lined up half a dozen possible sites for the Canadian branch of our Pharos International Corporation, two of them being in Toronto.

I was convinced in my own mind that the office should be in Montreal and showered Otto Guynemer with my reasons. To my surprise and relief he finally agreed with me so we surveyed the four available sites in Montreal.

It was accepted that my main duties while based in Canada would be concerned with checking the progress of our legitimate businesses and pushing our huge money-laundering system to the best of my ability.

Angelo's main task was supervising the movements of our very large drug shipments, mainly heroin, through the local traffickers en route to the United States.

Angie, being a born Sicilian mafioso with extensive experience in USA and other countries was ideally suited for this job. He knew the Cosa Nostra dialects, he knew their customs and he knew their attitudes. He was also very difficult to scare!

The money-laundering racket would involve close co-operation with Otto and Luigi. It must be remembered that Luigi was the final recipient of huge amounts of cash from our European enterprises and he would obviously prefer to hand it over to a trusted colleague for processing. Normally a risky business!

Eventually the four of us, Otto, Luigi, Angelo and me, decided that one of my selected sites for our Pharos International Corporation was suitable for our requirements.

Although it was a strictly legal company we needed a private office for the use of us guys when we visited the company as boss directors. An inner sanctum where snooping eyes could not peer and out of the earshot of curious staff members.

Remember that our knowledgeable spouses were also company directors and, being somewhat attractive specimens, their advent at the new company branch would be bound to attract attention from the fresh staff, mainly of local origin.

We purchased the office site which answered our requirements and Otto instructed me to supervise the furnishing of the offices. He gave me the basic layout which he considered suitable and told me to complete the furnishing before interviewing staff.

Again he would compile the advertisements for staff and would arrange for a senior manager from the London head office to come to Canada and co-operate with me in the interviewing procedure. The London executive would also undertake the initial staff training and stay on the job until Otto returned to start business rolling.

As the London man would be living on the job in Montreal I was given the task of finding him suitable housing.

Thus I had to walk the tightrope between performing my criminal operations and acting as a respectable company executive in cahoots with the guy from London, England.

When this peaceful interlude was completed we discussed with Luigi our suggested procedure for taking over the drug and associated rackets in Canada.

My aim was to convince the others that we should embroil Nicolo Rizzoli in our trade and gradually lure him to operate in direct opposition to the accepted big boss Vincenzo Cotillo. This would also include further antagonizing Paolo Velio, Cotillo's second in command. The latter requirement would not be difficult to arrange as Nicolo and Paolo currently hated each others guts. This was partly engendered because Nicolo was a very traditional Sicilian mafioso while Paolo was basically a 'ndrangheta clansman from Calabria on the Italian mainland. He was also an arrogant lout.

My colleagues did not need me to convince them on this part of our strategy as we had performed similar sequences in Europe during our take-over operations to enlarge our drug and vice rackets on that continent.

So we agreed on our procedure *vis-à-vis* Nicolo Rizzoli when he and his wife came to dinner at my place. It had been our habit to arrange consequential occasions well in advance and in detail so that we were all aware of expected results or possible snags which could develop.

These important occasions had included, over many years, everything from meetings with prospects to bloody massacres. The current discussion dealt with meeting a prospect. The massacre would be considered at the appropriate time!

Firdaussi arranged the dinner party in her customary expensive fashion by employing the up-market home caterer Quebec Haute Cuisine Services. We wanted a top class function to impress Nicolo and his spouse and, of course, for our own pleasure!

We intended to act in a very friendly manner to our guests and leave Luigi to broach, in private, the subject of nullifying the Cotillo supremacy in the local rackets.

Luigi, being a leading Cosa Nostra family don from Sicily, would be acceptable to the tradition loving Sicilian mafioso Nicolo Rizzoli. Especially when Luigi would be hinting at future benefits in finance and status for Nicolo and his family.

At this stage, obviously, Luigi would not be disclosing that finally he himself would be the top boss in Canada. Nor that he would not, repeat not, be subservient to the Bonnano crime family in New York as was the Cotillo cartel.

In other words, our murderous bunch of accomplished thugs were preparing to dominate the Canadian crime scene, as we were dominating Europe, by violence and intimidation.

Trouble was brewing in the form of a bloody turf war.

* * * * *

CHAPTER EIGHT

LAUNDERING THE PELF

Our various schemes slid into place smoothly due to much detailed planning in advance.

Our first drug shipment was brought in to Montreal, taken off our cargo boat and transported to New York by Vincenzo Cotillo's organization.

The senior executive from the London head office of Pharos International Corporation, a guy called John Norris, arrived with his wife and did all that he was hired to do, as ordered by Otto Guynemer.

I had purchased, on mob money, a decent apartment in a Montreal condominium for the couple to move into. Ensuring it was not situated too close to our houses to avoid jeopardizing our privacy.

To emphasize our spurious trust in Nicolo Rizzoli we took pains to slide a minor portion of our first drug shipment to his eager grasp. This, as stated, was part of our nefarious plot to use Nicolo and his family to oust Vincenzo Cotillo from his current leadership of the Canadian drug trafficking scene.

We soon received payment for our first load of narcotics and this added to my responsibilities as I had been delegated by our bosses, Otto Guynemer and Luigi Ferraro, to operate our money-laundering system.

This meant much travel and incrementation of numerous quasi-commercial companies in many countries. Luckily I had my wife Firdaussi to assist me in this task; luckily because she was a very astute business woman who knew as much about the rackets as I did.

Being a smart cookie she told me, "We'll treat our travels as vacations, Deac; if we're going to risk life and limb for our mob we are going to enjoy our time together all over the globe and I am sure Otto and Luigi will agree to that!"

Such like jocularity from a Persian bint, brought up in her

childhood in conditions of dire poverty and guided into prostitution at an early age to keep the family from starvation.

She sure had changed in the ensuing years!

* * * * *

An early problem in picking up our first drug money in Montreal was how to receive the very large amounts of cash, mostly in USA dollars, from our mafia purchasers without being noticed by inquisitive official eyeballs.

It was obvious to us that police anti-drug squads, the Inland Revenue agents, Customs officers and sundry other snooping groups would be watching the movements of known criminals like Vincenzo Cotillo, and Paolo Velio at least sporadically if not constantly.

Our aim was to avoid recognition by the authorities as accomplices of the local mobsters.

Hence we were not dumb enough to amble in to Cotillo's or Nicolo's headquarters and come out to our car carrying half a dozen large sacks of dollar bills.

However, Firdaussi and I, together with Angelo and spouse Maria, were savoring good Italian cuisine at one of our favorite eateries, the Ristorante Palladia in downtown Montreal while quietly discussing this knotty problem.

To our faint surprise Maria came up with a likely solution. I say faint surprise because although Maria was more than street wise she rarely produced earth shattering gems of wisdom.

This is how she put it, " When these guys inform us that they have our hard cash ready for collection we obviously don't intend to collect it because of the possibility of prying official eyes."

Maria paused briefly and took a hearty swig from her glass of Valpolicella vino.

I lit her a cigarette, she took a puff and continued, "So we don't collect the dough but we let them deliver it."

I butted in with, "If they deliver it then the goddamned cops can still follow them and check their delivery point. What the hell's the advantage of that?"

Maria surveyed me with kindly patience.

"Deacon," she replied, "I have been thinking of Nicolo Rizzoli, during our dinner party for his benefit, telling us that his son, Vittorio is a motor-cycle nut with a couple of Harley Davidsons in his backyard. So I have wondered, Vittorio being a mob member like his Dad, whether he could pick up our cash surreptitiously and deliver it to some quiet spot out of town where we could meet him and collect it. If a cop car tried to follow a crack motor-cyclist like Vittorio, especially through heavy traffic, they would lose him very rapidly. What do you all think of that?"

On first thoughts we thought it was a brilliant scheme. On second thoughts and after discussing the likely snags involved at some length we decided it remained a brilliant scheme. At least none of us could think up a better one.

So, I guess, after our congratulations and compliments, Maria now considered she was one of the brains of the mob as she basked in her moment of glory!

Be that as it may, I immediately asked Angelo to contact Nicolo Rizzoli and get him to fix it with his son to be our money courier.

We quit Ristorante Palladia and returned home, the four of us to my place. Angie reached Nicolo Rizzoli on the blower and requested a prompt interview to discuss a business matter. Nicolo agreed to see Angie and me right away at his Pizzeria Romano in Rue Jean-Talon.

So Angie and I set off in my Cadillac and were soon discussing the point in question with Nicolo. He thought Maria's idea would be a very good move and wondered why the hell he hadn't thought of it himself!

To clinch the arrangement he phoned Vittorio to come to the pizzeria. Vittorio arrived in quick time, having obeyed his Don's call by belting over on one of his Harleys.

Vittorio, having been put in the picture concerning the scheme, was only too glad to be doing something important and active on behalf of Cosa Nostra. He listened to our instructions very carefully and did not need to be reminded that when he picked up our large amounts of cash he could well be under the surveillance of a law enforcement group. Meaning that he would have to lose any following vehicles by using the flexibility and speed of his motor-cycle.

To test the scheme it was agreed that at 11am next day Vittorio would collect the cash that Nicolo owed us for his share of our first narcotics shipment to Montreal, stow it in the voluminous carriers on his Harley and rendezvous with our Buick convertible at a selected point far out of town, where Firdaussi and Maria would take it from him, put it on the back seat or in the trunk and take off for home. Mission accomplished!

We pored over a local map and agreed on a suitable rendezvous point out in the sticks. As far away from inquisitive eyes as we could imagine.

So we all went home but not before reminding Nicolo and son Vittorio that if all went well on our test run it would be necessary to inform Vincenzo Cotillo, the so-called Cosa Nostra boss in Canada, that we would want the same system to apply to the regular deliveries of the loads of cash which he owed and would continue to owe our cartel for the large drug shipments we were sending him from Europe.

We did not suggest that Nicolo should inform Cotillo personally; we would do that as we were aware of a certain hostility between Nicolo and Cotillo's underboss Paolo Velio which, at present, we did not wish to accelerate into active warfare.

Later perhaps when it suited our purpose?!

* * * * *

We approached Vincenzo Cotillo and explained our motor-cycle scheme, operated by Vittorio, for transferring the drug money to us. He thought it was a clever idea and agreed wholeheartedly to follow our instructions on pick-up days.

What the ever glowering Paolo Velio thought I could not guess and did not care to know.

I had a mental list of guys unsuitable for inclusion in our future aspirations. Paolo led the list.

However, we started to receive our cash without undue problems. We stored it in my abode and pondered on our next move.

During our period in Cairo, Egypt, we had laundered our

loads of illegally earned cash by flying them to Lebanon in our own aircraft and landing surreptitiously on a scrubby flat patch inland from Beirut, the capital city. Our cars were ready to take the cash back to a crooked banker in Beirut while I took off and landed normally at the international airport.

The banker, for a ten per cent consideration, would place phoney orders on our highly legal North Delta Trading Corporation based in Cairo. We accepted and processed these spurious orders with equally phoney paper work. After which the banker paid us for his orders in real money which went into our company accounts. These accounts were never queried by the local Inland Revenue inspectors because they appeared very legal!

And that's how Firdaussi and I made our first fortunes, even though we were then minor members of the Otto/ Luigi cartel.

Of course we were currently laundering our cash for the money we were receiving from our European operations so we were not beginners in the business.

In fact as Firdaussi and I were setting up a system to handle our receipts in Canada we would be in close touch with Otto Guynemer and Luigi Ferraro. They would want to know every proposed move in advance to ensure we were doing nothing to endanger our clean criminal records with law authorities worldwide.

Our intention was to register numerous commercial companies in various countries and pass our loot from one to another in such a complicated fashion as to make it very difficult for any snooping anti-drug squad officer to trace the eventual destination. Naturally we would not register the companies with our names as owners.

Luigi had scores of relatives, male and female, in Sicily who would willingly allow their lord and master, Don Luigi, to use their names for any purpose he wished. At the same time feeling grateful to be of service to the head of their mafia family.

So what with Luigi's family, certain of our trusted cohorts in Europe and our old friend and colleague, Abdul Mahmoud, in Egypt we would not be short of a name or names with which to register our new companies.

We decided that we would start our new deal in Liechtenstein. Why Liechtenstein? Because we were well aware that this country was "free enterprise" to the maximum. Cash from any source was accepted by certain leading banking specialists with no questions asked except, "What's in it for us?!"

Otto Guynemer had put me in touch with Dr. Albert Klesinger, a legal and financial professional, who would register a "paper" company name to which we could wire or deliver cash. This money would then be transmitted to Switzerland through the willing co-operation of a money-laundering bank in Liechtenstein, well used by the worthy Dr. Klesinger.

By coincidence (!) our cartel already had a secret and legal Swiss bank account which we had arranged years before when our mob quit Cairo, Egypt. And we had left some six million pounds sterling in that account. A very useful sum which our Sicilian gang had put away to cover future emergencies. And all very legal and explainable!

So Firdaussi and I set off for Liechtenstein to meet Albert Klesinger personally and make concrete arrangements. Including, as you may have already surmised, ensuring that our "paper" company or companies, would not be registered in our names.

Luigi, in Sicily, had supplied us with the names of some of his family members who, naturally, had no objection to their Don using their names as he thought fit.

We flew to Zurich, Switzerland, complete with extensive luggage including one trunk containing some holiday gear and also half a million US dollars in cash.

We took a slight chance on this being questioned by inquisitive Customs officers but had little fear of further official action because, after all, both Firdaussi and I were directors of a prominent international enterprise, namely Pharos International Corporation.

Surely such trusted executive officers were entitled to transport company money to their special account in Switzerland?! And, in my pocket, was written authority to do this very thing signed by the company president, Mr. Otto Guynemer.

Anyway, off we went to Liechtenstein by rail in a very comfortable private apartment on an efficiently run Swiss train. The fifty miles to our destination were covered rapidly and we taxied to the resplendent Hotel Wunderbar, probably one of the ten top up-market hotels in Europe where we had booked a suite in advance.

We settled in comfortably and headed for the dining hall, leaving our five-hundred grand ensconced in the trunk.

Were we worried about security of our cash?

Not very much. Firdy and I were more concerned with getting a good lunch!

Our casual attitude was engendered by the knowledge, from past experience, that, even if our load of cash vanished during lunch-time there was plenty more where that came from!

We enjoyed a leisurely and excellent meal followed by coffees and liqueur.

Then back to our suite where we enjoyed a leisurely and excellent session in the king-size bed. After which we showered and cleaned up before we deigned to get back to business.

After all, our bosses had told us to act as if we were on holiday!

I 'phoned our target, Doctor Albert Klesinger, got his address and learned from him that he was eager to meet us.

Off we sallied, by taxi, toting our trunk of cash. The word "trunk" might imply it was a large heavy piece of equipment. It was more a larger type of valise, not too bulky to carry personally.

We met the affable and charmingly respectable big-time crook, Dr. Klesinger, in his imposing office where he made us welcome, gave us drinks and smokes before getting down to business.

He spoke near perfect English, answered our relevant questions and asked us a few of his own. Firdaussi, who even after years of intimacy between us, I still suspected was smarter than me, was far from backward in placing her queries.

The doctors eyes lit up when I opened our valise and told him how much cash it contained. He took our word for the amount of cash therein and we took his word he would process it as required. We did not ask for a receipt as he knew we represented a powerful Sicilian mafia cartel and was aware that we did not treat dishonest colleagues leniently. On top of which he was getting a useful percentage of our input to his system.

We learned the names of two local banks who co-operated with the doctor on money laundering for the drug barons and we also learned that our new acquaintance was secretly banking illegal gains for many eminent political leaders in numerous countries around the world including a couple of presidents and high ranking churchmen.

We finished our meeting by asking Albert, as we now called him, to dinner at our hotel, including of course his female partner who was not yet his official wife.

He accepted our offer graciously, probably thinking it would give him further opportunity to assess his new clients.

I reported by 'phone to Otto Guynemer as soon as we returned to our hotel, using one of the public telephones kiosked in the reception area. Using our room 'phone would allow the hotel operator to listen in to our conversation.

Otto was pleased at our progress and said he would contact Luigi in Sicily and pass on the news. He told us to return to Canada and check on our matters there while supporting Angelo and Maria if they needed any assistance in their local work.

After which we were to proceed on the next stage of our money laundering project.

* * * * *

CHAPTER NINE

FURTHER TRAVEL

Before returning to Montreal we decided to do a little sight seeing in Liechtenstein and Switzerland.

We spent nearly a week seeing the sights at Luzern, Lausanne, the mighty Alps and generally enjoying ourselves before boarding a jet at Zurich to return to Canada.

Refreshed after completing our business with Dr. Klesinger we got down to business in Montreal.

We contacted Angelo and Maria, had a long discussion about progress with the Cotillo mob after which we checked our Pharos International Corporation branch and were pleased to learn it was handling a contract with a provincial government and another with a major City Council way over in British Columbia. So our legal salaries were secure!

Now back to our illegal affairs.

Angelo, due to his increasingly close contacts with the Cotillo and Nicolo Rizzoli groups in Montreal had discovered that it could be worth our while to have a close look at Venezuela in connection with our money-laundering operation.

We pondered on this suggestion and made a few local inquiries to further our knowledge.

During a dinner with Nicolo Rizzoli and his wife we found out, after broaching the question cautiously, that he was convinced that certain high level officials in Venezuela would not be averse to a reasonable back-hander for services rendered.

With this knowledge I suggested to our bosses in Europe that we, Firdaussi and me, should visit Venezuela and check out the prospects.

After a few days enjoying ourselves with our old friends Angelo and Maria we were told to go to Venezuela and do what we considered necessary to further our activities.

Having surmised that this would be our instructions we had prepared ourselves and booked our air flight to Caracas, capital city of Venezuela.

Before taking off we had made sure that our order to the top hotel for their best suite had been wired and accepted.

In our now habitual way we were determined never to be poor and uncomfortable again!

After landing at the airport and completing the not very stringent Immigration and Customs formalities we taxied to the Sanspareil Hotel where we made ourselves comfortable and went down to try out the cuisine.

It was delectable and we lingered over our meal while discussing our next moves.

Our first business move next morning was to contact a couple of realtors. We intended to set up another office of our highly legal company Pharos International Corporation and quietly use it in our money laundering operations.

In effect it would be a "paper" company, the "employees" would be members of our boss's Sicilian mafia family who would be imported to act as caretakers under our strict control. This arrangement had, of course, been arranged with Luigi before we had left Montreal.

It must be remembered that although Angelo, Maria, Firdaussi and I were long time members of the Sicilian cartel and were entrusted with wide discretion in our criminal affairs we all performed our functions under the basic planning of Otto Guynemer and Luigi Ferraro and had accepted this willingly for many years, most of them very hectic and lucrative years!

One of our selected realtors soon came up with some sites which we could consider for our new office.

Firdaussi and I trekked around the town with this guy for a couple of boring days until, at last we discovered a suitable site for Pharos International Corporation branch office in South America. On top of this we had to find some decent accommodation for the staff. The pseudo staff, of course, being half-dozen reliable members of Luigi Ferraro's Sicilian mafia family.

To assist us in meeting these types and communicating with them, as our basic Italian did not include Sicilian dialects, I wired Angelo in Montreal, Quebec, and asked him to visit Caracas.

Angie, being Luigi's mafia underboss, would be able to converse with and give instructions to the newcomers which they would obey to the letter.

We picked some very good class accommodation for our new boys and girls. Yes, two of them were bringing their spouses.

We did not forget to book a suite in our hotel for Angelo and Maria who arrived in Caracas within two days of my wire being sent. The new Pharos International Corporation "staff" were not long behind them.

They appeared to be an intelligent crowd and I hoped they would soon pick up enough Venezuelan Spanish to get by.

To the delight of our realtor we promptly bought the office site in the name of the Pharos headquarters in London and the residential accommodation in the names of their mafia occupants!

We then had to get official permission to register Pharos as a functioning business. I completed all the necessary forms and had to attend an interview with the government officer in charge of the commercial department.

I sensed that this influential official was affable, over affable, for a reason so, with Deacon Roy's long experience of crooks at all levels, I invited him and his wife to a lavish dinner at our top market hotel.

My stratagem did not fail.

Our official dropped a not so subtle hint, in English (!), that a reasonable fee would expedite our business and a regular reasonable fee would not only prevent any official interference with Pharos but might help grease the fingers of the local tax inspector, who worked hand in glove with our dinner guest.

I soon arranged a more than reasonable regular fee which made the recipient's eyes sparkle and ensured we could use Pharos International Corporation, Caracas, Venezuela, in our money-laundering operations with comparative safety.

We stayed in Caracas while we trained the new staff of Pharos in their money laundering duties. Angie's natural ability to converse in their Sicilian dialect was of inestimable value.

Their duties were quite simple in effect. We set up bank accounts in all their names and a couple more for the Pharos company. They were instructed to telephone me or Angelo in Montreal, Canada, when sums of money were wired by us to these bank accounts and were registered therein. On receipt of these sums being confirmed we would inform them what to do next. This would generally mean that these sums, or portions of them, would be wired in their turn to our legal Pharos accounts in Switzerland or to our phoney "paper" companies in Liechtenstein. One advantage we enjoyed with our spurious Liechtenstein companies was that we could obtain "loans" from these firms, thus borrowing our own money and not having to worry about the rate of interest! Very convenient and apparently legal.

It may be instructive at this point to state that there were certain banks in Montreal where we could pay in our large quantities of illegal drug cash without questions being asked.

Why this should be may be explained by the fact that the managers of these banks had been individually invited to dine with us in our customary style. Apart from the banks officially charging considerable fees for their services, the managers were more than friendly on receipt of a reasonable fee of their very own.

We had numerous accounts at these banks, all of them being registered to even more members of Luigi's family in Sicily!

Not registered, you will doubtless have noticed, to us, the Good Ol' Boys!

In addition our highly legal company, Pharos International Corporation, had accounts in each of these chosen banks. An added refinement which could be useful to our crooked tactics when necessary.

As a protective maneuver we arranged for our loads of US dollars to be paid in by Vittorio, the motor-cycling son of Nicolo Rizzoli, who, as stated previously, already collected our drug money from local boss Vincenzo Cotillo.

Vittorio, with his Dad's agreement, was eager to undertake this added responsibility as it substantially increased his personal income and made him feel more of a real mafioso.

So we were setting up a system where we, the old mob, were hopefully remote from apparent personal involvement in money laundering, even though we controlled the set-up with an iron hand when necessary.

And the iron hand was going to be necessary in the not too distant future.

The reason being that Paolo Velio, underboss to Vincenzo Cotillo was being even more obnoxious than usual and his target was our new acquaintance Nicolo Rizzoli.

Our sources told us that he had gone to New York to get the

controlling Bonnano family to permit him to eradicate Nicolo Rizzoli by lethal force.

Hearing this Nicolo took off for Aruba, a self-governing Dutch island in the Caribbean.

Previous to this self-protective flight by our friend, Firdaussi and I had been ordered to move to Aruba by our bosses, Otto and Luigi, in order to set up viable businesses.

These businesses would be earning us money legally as well as fitting in with our money laundering activities. This latter function was made simpler by the highly confidential banking system which almost put the island on a par with Liechtenstein for the benefit of criminal groups with money to hide from snooping officialdom.

* * * * *

CHAPTER TEN

MEYER LANSKY

However, after our sojourn in the isle of Aruba, we, to our great surprise, were instructed to visit our old friend Santos Salvatore in Miami, Florida.

Surprised because we had been warned not to visit the United States after our cataclysmic assassination foray in Dallas, Texas, engineered basically by Santos Salvatore.

Our bosses must have considered the initial FBI heat had reduced somewhat.

Be that as it may we met Santos in Miami when he told us the objective behind our trip. We were to travel to Las Vegas, Nevada, book in at the Flamingo hotel and ask for Meyer Lanski, who we were informed, "Was a financial genius to the mob."

On our arrival at the Flamingo we were impressed by the size of the place and found that apart from being a luxury hotel it included a casino and entertainment center. It was really sucker bait for the willing tourist with money.

We booked in to a sumptuous suite on the top floor with a wonderful view of the arid desert which did not impress us. We cleaned up and made ourselves comfortable before descending to the main reception desk and asking for Meyer Lansky.

We were informed that Lansky would meet us for a discussion in his apartment, also on the top floor.

Back in the express elevator which shot us upwards at high velocity and we soon found Lansky's apartment.

He welcomed us with great affability and soon put us at our ease. I could tell he was a very persuasive gentleman.

We discovered that his parents were Polish Jews and that he was currently investing in hotels, casinos, golf clubs and businesses where the audience gave up their money willingly if you supplied the right environment for their enjoyment.

However, to pursue his preoccupation with investment needed immediate financial resources. Having his ear close to the ground in the organized crime underworld he was aware that our Sicilian cartel was being flooded with vast amounts of cash from our European and North American ventures.

"In short, Deacon, how much can your organization lend me on a fixed rate of interest, repayment guaranteed in part or whole in five to seven years?"

Firdaussi answered for me while I was still pondering on Meyer Lansky's statement.

"Meyer", she started, "What kind of guarantee can we rely on?"

"You have my solemn word," he replied, "What can I do better than that?

Now it was my turn. "Meyer," I broke in, "Don't imagine we don't trust your solemn word. I have been authorized to lend initially up to fifty million US dollars and I don't intend to inform my bosses that I have accepted your repayment guarantee by word of mouth only.

In addition to your solemn word of honor I must have a more solid sort of guarantee. Have you any suggestions, Meyer?"

I could tell from Lansky's expression that my remarks about an initial loan of up to fifty million dollars had impressed him because it suggested there could be more to follow if he needed it. But I knew he would not want to give too much away.

So did my bright wife Firdy.

"Meyer," she interposed, paused, continued, "Meyer, I feel our organization would be happy to furnish your loan in controlled amounts to pay for each investment as it occurs.

In other words you get the money you require whenever you need it. The other point, the guarantee, would be ensured by our joint participation in each of your future investment projects. Our participation in the project would be of comparatively minor degree, including a seat on the board of directors, leaving you in full control of the business."

Meyer Lansky's serious expression broke into a genuine smile as he surveyed us quizzically.

" Where did you guys learn about big business," he chortled. "You certainly know all the right answers and I accept your stipulations about minor participation. I am willing to put this agreement in legal form supervised by an attorney. Now lets go to eat dinner when I 'll tell you how soon I want the first piece of my loan."

We all rose, relieved that our expected tough interview had finalized so smoothly and were escorted by the formidable Meyer Lansky to the elevator and hence to the dining hall and a grand dinner as his guests.

I reported our achievement to Otto Guynemer who was at his estate in England. He said we were to accept Lansky's legal agreement by the attorney and then wire ten million dollars to his bank account from one of our "paper" companies in Liechtenstein.

Our stated interest rate was to be modest because with our participation we would have a share of any profits made by Lansky's future projects.

Otto was convinced that Meyer Lansky would repay us as soon as he could. "In spite of his early background, Deacon, Meyer is a honest man!" said Otto.

After sorting out the essential details while we lived in luxury at the Flamingo Hotel we said goodbye to Meyer Lansky and headed for our next stop, Aruba, yet again.

* * * * *

CHAPTER ELEVEN

THE FRUITFUL ISLAND - ARUBA

We soon detected the Dutch influence in Aruba. Although under the jurisdiction of the Netherlands authorities it was, in fact, a self-governing island in the Caribbean with a population of approximately fifty thousand people.

An advantage to us was that most of the individuals we contacted on business spoke English. This ability seems to be a common asset with Dutch citizens. It appears to have rubbed off on the inhabitants of Dutch Aruba.

The first business action performed was to set up several bank accounts in a variety of banks. Most of these accounts were in the names of Luigi's mafia family members but two of them were in our own names, these two were for legal cash deposits. When I say "legal" I mean successfully laundered criminal receipts from our drug and other rackets.

It was not difficult setting up these accounts because, as stated previously, the Aruba banking system was very accommodating for people like us.

Our bosses had instructed us to survey various types of businesses in Aruba with a view to buying them after checking their profitability. We were to report our findings to Otto and Luigi who would assess our suggestions and if agreement was reached would give us the OK to purchase.

Apart from the legal profits obtained the purchased companies would be of great assistance in our money-laundering activities.

The cash required for each purchase would be wired to one of our bank accounts in Aruba from a "paper" company of ours in Liechtenstein.

If our group was unfortunate enough to fall foul of some snooping government agency they would have one hell of a job tracing our cash flow. Which, of course, was the object of our labors!

So Firdaussi and I contacted realtors and checked sundry firms including hotels, resorts, casinos, gas stations and any apparently lucrative business which would fit our requirements. Even the realtors who were escorting us in our search!

We had a vast amount of illicit cash pouring into our coffers so we had to put it somewhere safe.

Our first agreed purchase was a large, tourist popular hotel/resort with all the trimmings, pool, casino and so on.

Naturally we did not purchase this bit of real estate blindly. We hired a top group of chartered accountants, all Dutch citizens, who we considered were trustworthy, to check the accounts and profitability of this resort.

On receiving their assessment, which was positive, we made an offer to the owners which they could not refuse. So our Sicilian mob became the proud owners of this highly popular luxury hotel, casino and tourist resort, even though, on paper, the property was owned by one of our phony Liechtenstein companies.

Again naturally, Firdy and I moved in to the best top floor suite and lived the life of Riley! Our hotel employed the top chefs in Aruba so we knew our meals would be up to our now accepted standard.

After this initial purchase our boss Luigi Ferraro decided to visit Aruba with his wife Tania to see what his cohorts (us!) were up to. We had no trouble accommodating them in another luxury suite in our posh hotel and were relieved to discover that Luigi, after thorough investigation, considered we had done well.

* * * * *

We were enjoying a good dinner together with Luigi and his wife Tania when, to my surprise, almost to my astonishment, I noticed a man and his wife being escorted to a table and, not only did I know them, the man was the same fellow that our mob intended to instal as leader of the Montreal rackets.

It was the ambitious mafioso Nicolo Rizzoli in person!

I rapidly drew the attention of my colleagues to this fact and Luigi responded just as rapidly, "Go over and invite them to join us, Deac."

So I went over and asked the astonished couple to join us at our table. Which they did.

After the customary hand-shakes and affability Nicolo, still somewhat stunned after what was to him our abrupt appearance, asked, "What the hell are you guys doing here?" Adding apologetically, "If I may ask such a personal question?"

We realized that the seasoned traditional mafioso was under a bit of stress so we accepted his query with understanding smiles.

I started off with, " Nicolo, before answering your question I must inform you that you are in our property and you will no doubt be pleased to know that your accommodation and meals in this establishment will be free, gratis and for nothing!"

Luigi took over, " Before we give out any more info, Nicolo, tell us what the hell you are doing here!"

Nicolo looked a little uncomfortable at Luigi's curt query so, as a waiter was hovering around Nicolo and his wife expectantly, Firdaussi suggested they should give their orders and ask for an aperitif each. This gave Nicolo time to regain his normal composure. Clever Firdy!

Nicolo soon put us in the picture. " We're here because I'm on the run from Canada. You know that pig Paolo Velio, underboss of Vincenzo Cotillo, has always hated my guts?" He paused to emphasise what we already knew.

He continued, " Well he's now gone the whole hog, He has visited the Bonnano family in New York, convinced them that I am a menace to the system and got their permission to have me whacked at the earliest opportunity.

So, to save my skin we left Montreal in a hurry and came here incognito. Our son, Vittorio, is following rapidly as he could be in danger from that fat swine too."

Nicolo sipped his aperitif and looked around the table to see what effect his disclosure had made on his listeners.

Luigi, like the rest of us, had rapidly assessed the situation.

" We get the picture, Nicolo," he responded, " And we have a solution to your problem which is going to fit in nicely with our future plans in Canada."

He took a drag from his Lucky Strike and continued, "After dinner we will all go up to Deacon's apartment and discuss this matter in private. In the meantime we will concentrate on enjoying our meal."

Luigi grinned, stubbed his Lucky and took a sip of his aperitif.

Things in Montreal were moving to our advantage.

* * * * *

Our conversation during our leisurely meal did not include any mention of Nicolo's problem. We chatted about this and that while outlining our actual and future business purchases in Aruba for Nicolo's information.

On finishing our coffee and liqueurs we rose and ambled out of the dining area to a convenient elevator.

I signaled the maitre d'hotel, told him to put the bill for our table on my account then joined the others as the elevator arrived at our level.

We soon shot up to the top floor and did not take long to make ourselves comfortable in our suite. There was a plentiful supply of drinks which were doled out by Firdaussi and Tania before we got down to business.

Luigi addressed Nicolo directly as the rest of us knew what Luigi had in mind. The fact that Nicolo's wife was included did not worry us as we were well aware that mafia wives knew the rules about keeping the mouth shut!

"Nicolo," Luigi opened his spiel, "Nicolo, we understand your present unfortunate circumstances but they have occurred at a very opportune moment, a moment our cartel has planned ever since we came to Montreal.

You know for sure that most of our drug shipments into Canada are collected by Vincenzo Cotillo's outfit and passed over the border to the Bonnano family in New York. In fact a small share of each shipment of narcotics was allocated to you personally by us intentionally.

You, Nicolo, have a somewhat precarious connection with the Cotillo mob. Precarious since the death of Cotillo's underboss, Louis Gratto, and his replacement by Paolo Velio who has always hated your guts, Nicolo, and is now seeking the opportunity to blow you away. Deacon will give you an outline of our proposed action in Montreal in the near future."

Luigi nodded to me to carry on with the description of our future tactics.

I began, " Nicolo, from the start we envisaged taking over the drug racket from the Cotillo organization. Our normal business tactics are to avoid middle-men and deal direct with the distributors. The distributors in this case are those Sicilian elements in the Bonnano crime family in New York who are drug dealers.

In our eyes Cotillo is a middle-man pure and simple. He and his mob take a cut out of the Bonnano family drug repayments which should come to us. And what do they do to earn that cut? Nothing that an intelligent chimpanzee couldn't do!"

Nicolo Rizzoli, his wife and even my own colleagues, chortled at my remark.

I continued, "To take over the Cotillo system will necessitate the removal of Paolo Velio and his close accomplices. We feel that the removal of that fat pig will preclude the need to get rid of Vincenzo Cotillo in like manner. We understand he is suffering a serious health problem which will probably soon kill him.

When our Sicilian cartel decides to remove opponents we do not ask permission from any mafia family or group of mafia families. We eliminate them in our own well-tested fashion."

I paused in order to let my words sink in and took the opportunity to light up one of Luigi's Luckies and take a swig of my Pilsener beer.

Nicolo Rizzoli broke in, " My friends, you may or may not know that the fat pig has two very close accomplices who support his every action.

One is his brother Flavio Velio and the other is Pietro Caselli, adviser and clever enough to take over if the fat pig is eliminated.

To further ease your take-over in Canada these two would have to go."

Luigi took over with, "Nicolo, have you enough scope to funnel our complete narcotics shipments to the United States and the ability to persuade the Bonnano family drug section to pay the cash to you instead of Vincenzo Cotillo?

Remembering that the Bonnano family gave the fat pig permission to knock you off?"

Nicolo replied without hesitation, "I have long thought about taking over the Cotillo organization and have considered the many problems and how best to find their solutions.

The big problem occurred when Cotillo made the dumb decision to make Paolo Velio his underboss.

A dumb decision because Paolo is a fat, domineering and lethally violent slob of the first magnitude as well as being a 'ndrangheta clansman from Calabria with a built-in contempt for our families from Sicily.

Yes. I could handle your large shipments of dope satisfactorily if we can eliminate our chief opponents."

Luigi interposed, "Good, we thought you could do it , Nicolo. You will appreciate that we intended to take charge of the major rackets in Canada even before we met you.

Since getting to know you we feel that your inclusion will speed up the operation.

When we decide to remove the opposition it is obvious that you will be suspected, by police and Cosa Nostra, as the guy most likely to have organized the slaughter.

We are suggesting that you and your wife remain in Aruba until we inform you that the fat pig and his cohorts have been removed. Making sure in the meantime that you are well in the public eye as alibi that you were not involved in the shooting.

You then fly back to Montreal and take over what remains of the Cotillo outfit and reorganize it to our satisfaction."

Luigi stopped his spiel to ask Tania to get him another glass of Bourbon and probably to give Nicolo time to digest his words.

Firdaussi, being nearer the drinks cabinet motioned to Tania that she would get Luigi's Bourbon as well as another beer for me.

Luigi lit yet another Lucky Strike, swigged his whiskey and continued his address to Nicolo.

" You will appreciate, Nicolo, that our action in Montreal will make our cartel the Cosa Nostra bosses in Canada?"

Luigi made a query out of his statement and I noticed his expression hardened. He had become the flint-eyed, grim faced mafia hit-man that I knew of old. He was Don Luigi Ferraro, controlling a powerful and very wealthy crime cartel. His success in life was due to two influences: No conscience and the gun!

He carried on, "You will also appreciate, Nicolo, that if we put you in charge of our Canadian interests you will not only become very wealthy but will be under our control and will receive help from us as required. In fact Deacon and Angelo will be in Canada to assist in your initial take over of our Montreal system and your personal status and image as the apparent big boss will not be affected.

This offer is, of course, confidential and I will give you until tomorrow to ponder on it.

If you accept, Nicolo, I will want you to swear, as a traditional mafia man of honor, that only death will release you from your bond."

With that Luigi ceased his peroration, the rasp left his voice and he returned to the convivial Luigi.

He suggested to me, "Deac, get on the blower and ask Room Service to send up some supper, chicken legs and snack stuff, with a few bottles of vino, Italiano,naturally!"

I did just that and Room Service, knowing we were the owners, soon delivered a choice variety of snacks plus half a dozen bottles including Barolo, Valpolicella and the like.

As we relaxed after our business discussion I noticed a few whispers and knowing nods and glances between Nicolo and his wife.

I guessed that with the intimacy engendered by a long and apparently successful marriage they were communicating quietly about Luigi's offer. I was sure that his wife, upset by the death threat to her husband, would be only too glad to have him under the protection of our Sicilian cartel, and, in effect, have the death threat removed without his physical involvement.

As for Nicolo himself? Any guy who turned down a once in a lifetime offer which would simultaneously remove his death sentence and bring him great wealth would certainly be a nut case.

I had just finished pouring six glasses of wine with Firdy passing them around as required when Nicolo said, very audibly, " I have something to say!"

There was immediate silence and Nicolo rose to his feet, looked straight at Luigi, slightly bowed his head in apparent respect and said, "Don Luigi Ferraro, I accept your recent offer and will swear the solemn mafia oath to serve your Cosa Nostra family to the best of my ability. I consider I am now under your orders." With another slight bow of respect he sat down.

Our short burst of hand-clapped applause was, I felt, due to relief in getting a reliable Sicilian mafioso of the old school on our books in Canada. It was going to save us one helluva lot of trouble. And we Good Ol' Boys would still be incognito to the authorities!

After that bit of ceremony we settled down to enjoy our suppers and swig our vino. Plus a few other drinks!

What then? The night was young and we had a flourishing casino down below.

So down we sallied and, slightly inebriated, I lost a lot of Aruba florins on the roulette wheel and shooting craps. My companions didn't do much better. Except my wife Firdy!

Firdaussi, as was usual during her occasional gambling sorties, made more money than I lost.

I don't suppose our losses mattered two hoots really because we were the owners of that goddamned casino!

* * * * *

Late next morning Nicolo's son Vittorio turned up at the hotel. We were expecting him as Nicolo had told us he wanted Vittorio out of Montreal because the fat man, Paolo Velio, was unstable enough to order Vittorio killed when he couldn't find his primary target, Nicolo.

However, Luigi had developed his own plan for future action and informed Firdaussi and me that we were returning to Montreal, that I was to contact Angelo and Maria in Caracas and tell them to head for Montreal immediately.

He also told Nicolo that Vittorio was to accompany us back to Canada as his assistance was needed in locating Paolo Velio when the time came.

So, leaving Nicolo and his spouse behind in our luxury hotel, we headed for the airport and soon took off for Toronto, Canada.

* * * * *

CHAPTER TWELVE

GOODBYE PAOLO!

On arrival at Toronto we picked up a hire car and were driven to our home in Montreal, Quebec, by Vittorio. Yes, he was a good car driver as well as being a nut on Harley-Davidson motor cycles!

Vittorio was told to return the hire car and come back on one of his Harleys because he was going to stay with us to ensure his security.

Angie and Maria soon joined us after their trip back from Caracas. As you know their home was near ours and it was arranged that Vittorio would bunk at their place while Luigi and Tania would stay with us.

Both our homes were quite large so we had no problems in putting people up as required.

As we had no wish to be seen with young Vittorio Rizzoli in public, at least at the moment, we decided to have dinner at a restaurant about half way along the road to St. Jerome rather than in down-town Montreal.

Vittorio was delighted to be included in our party because his Dad, Nicolo, had told him, during his visit to Aruba, about his new relationship vis-à-vis our Sicilian cartel.

It pleased Vittorio to know that the top brass in organized crime (us!) needed his assistance. He was aware that we had returned to Montreal for our next job, the forcible removal of our chief opponents.

So he was more than happy to drive us to our chosen restaurant in my Cadillac sedan.

In our usual manner we had a leisurely meal with all the trimmings. It was a German run restaurant which made a change and it was pleasant to be able to chose between a variety of good beers and some superb products of the Riesling grape. They went well with the excellent German cuisine.

It can be observed that wealth had engendered comprehensive tastes in our food and drink requirements.

Expensive tastes!

Vittorio managed to drive us home safely after our repast and we all bedded down gratefully after Luigi informed us we would discuss our future plans in the morning.

* * * * * *

After breakfast next morning, during our debate, Luigi mentioned our conversations with Nicolo Rizzoli in Aruba when it was emphasized that to take over the Cotillo organization it was not only necessary to remove the fat pig Paolo Velio.

There were two other guys with influence who backed every move made by Paolo Velio. They were Flavio Velio, his brother and his right hand man, Pietro Caselli. They both had to go.

Young Vittorio was pleased to discover that he had become a valuable member of our murder squad. Without his help and local knowledge our lethal plot would be delayed in its fruition.

The first essential was to obtain suitable weapons. It was decided that sub-machine guns were out of the question in our probable down-town target areas. The snags were the noise factor which could draw official attention and risk our desired anonymity plus the possibility of accidentally hitting innocent bystanders.

Yes, we really were worried about the latter possibility, but not because of conscience or feelings of humanity!

You kill a known racketeer and the local cops are not unduly worried, in fact they are often very pleased that one more nuisance has vanished!

You kill an innocent old lady, old gent, a nursing mother or a bright young student and the media really go to town. More than likely attracting political and federal investigators which could really be dangerous.

We asked Vittorio if he could obtain four pistols, three sawn-off shotguns and ammunition without attracting too much attention.

Vittorio told us that there were several un-registered firearms cached in his father's house. He would go there on his Harley and bring back anything suitable. The house was empty now his Mum and Dad were still in Aruba so there was nothing to delay his return. In any case, one of his friends made a living smuggling firearms into Canada from USA so any shortage of guns could soon be rectified.

Luigi sent Vittorio off on his gun finding mission. He returned within two hours and we laid out the arms on a bench in our convenient workshop.

There were two 12 gauge Remington shotguns; three semi-auto .45 caliber Colt pistols and two snub-nosed Smith and Wesson .357 magnum revolvers. A potent selection plus the requisite ammunition.

As usual, Luigi told the ex-armorer (me!) to thoroughly check the arms and shells. Also to saw off the shotgun barrels as we were not intending to shoot pheasants for sport!

I did this while the others returned to the lounge for a few drinks. The guns all functioned normally, they had hardly been used, if ever in most cases. Sawing off the shotgun barrels to a suitable length did not take long.

I rejoined the others and discovered the current topic concerned ascertaining the whereabouts of our prospective victims at the most suitable time.

It was suggested to Vittorio that he should drift around Montreal and meet as many of his young Sicilian mafia friends as possible and find out if local gossip gave a clue to Paolo Velio's habitual movements.

However it was emphasized by us that he was not to disclose to anybody that he was living with our group.

"Tell those guys who ask that you are living in your Dad's home as usual." ordered Luigi.

In addition to Vittorio's efforts we considered it a good idea to visit Vincenzo Cotillo and his underboss Paolo Velio to maintain business contact. While with them we might glean some information on Paolo's customary movements.

However, after our several boring talks with the Cotillo faction, it was Vittorio who came up with useful information.

He discovered that fat man Paolo Velio often went to play cards with a group of fellow Calabrian gangsters at the Regalo bar and social club on Rue Jeanne d'Arc, an establishment once owned by his hated opponent Nicolo Rizzoli, Vittorio's father!

Although Paolo Velio did not visit the Regalo bar on regular days he was often there at week ends from Friday evening onward. It was probably his only time for recreation. He was generally accompanied by his brother Flavio, who was probably acting as Paolo's bodyguard.

We had met Flavio several times during our social and business visits to the Cotillo group so Luigi, Angelo and I would have no difficulty in recognizing our victims on murder night.

It was decided that Vittorio would hire a car and transport us shooters to a parking spot where we could watch the door of the Regalo club. When we spotted our quarry enter the Regalo we would give them time to settle down before we moved.

Then we would don our cagoules to disguise our faces and Vittorio, who knew the layout of his Dad's old club, would lead us to the card players area and we would do what we had planned.

Angelo and I were to shotgun Paolo Vielo while Luigi pistoled Flavio to death. After the few seconds needed to perform our deadly work we would rapidly reload our shotguns and make our way out of the club to our car.

That was the general plan of action and Luigi decided we would start our first sojourn watching the Regalo bar entry the next day which was Friday.

* * * * *

Vittorio rented two hire cars from separate companies. He drove one with Luigi as his passenger and Angelo drove the other with me beside him. We parked near the scene of action where we could all see the entry to the Regalo club.

And waited.

We smoked and chewed gum for a boring half-hour until a big Lincoln sedan drew up in front of the club. Two men alighted and strolled to the door. The Lincoln driver drove away.

We hastily stubbed our cigarettes and prepared for action.

Our quarry had arrived!

After a ten minute wait Luigi gave us the signal to go. We ambled casually to the club entrance. Angie and I had our sawn-offs concealed under our trench coats.

Luigi motioned to Vittorio to take the lead and we entered the Regalo, putting on our cagoules as we increased our pace.

It didn't take us long to reach our quarries. There were several tables of card players and Paolo Velio was sitting on the farthest one, facing us, with his brother Flavio to the right of him.

We pushed between the tables without ceremony, guns in hand just as Flavio started dealing the first hand. He saw us and started to shout a warning to Paolo but it was too late.

We three shooters opened fire simultaneously and Flavio never finished his deal. Luigi shot him three times in the chest and blew him off his chair backwards.

Angie and I gave Paolo four loads of buckshot but he was too bulky to be blown backwards. He endeavored feebly to rise so Luigi gave him a couple more heavy .45 slugs and Paolo slid down grotesquely half under the table.

The card room was now in uproar. Players were panicking and diving under tables because they were unaware of our main targets, some of them probably thinking they were going to be included in the slaughter.

We three Good Ol' Boys had done this sort of execution many times before so were highly alert but absolutely unflappable.

After re-loading our weapons, a precaution in case some optimist tried to oppose our exit, we made our way to the door.

On reaching the street we whipped off our cagoules, hid our shotguns under our trench coats and rapidly reached our cars.

We drove away individually without haste, left our cars in convenient spots for Vittorio to pick up later before returning them to the renters, and returned to my abode in separate taxis.

Here we were welcomed by our spouses who, of course, were well aware of what we had been up to.

On being told that all was OK so far our wives informed us that we could now take them out to an expensive dinner.

So we men cleaned up and were then, together with our ladies, driven by Vittorio in my Cadillac to the Ristorante Palladia where we all enjoyed an exceedingly expensive meal without a second thought about the mayhem we had recently created at the Regalo bar.

Our murderous affray had taken about five seconds of gunfire so perhaps it was too minor an affair for us experts to ponder on!

CHAPTER THIRTEEN

WELCOME NICOLO

Vittorio was instructed by Luigi to fly to Aruba and tell his Dad that he should now return to Montreal and take over the narcotics racket from the Vincenzo Cotillo group.

"And emphasize that it will not be too difficult as somebody has removed that pig Paolo Velio permanently." Luigi concluded flippantly. Luigi was a great one for somber witticisms!

* * * * *

Nicolo Rizzoli returned to his home in Montreal with relief and satisfaction.

Relief because in Luigi's words, "Somebody has removed that pig Paolo Velio permanently!" and, of course, Vittorio had informed his Dad who "somebody" was (or were!).

Satisfaction because he knew he could use his own organization to promote the drug and vice rackets and be the big boss in Canada, albeit under the strict surveillance of our Sicilian cartel, the Good 'Ol Boys who punished indiscipline to finality, fatal finality!

However he discussed with our group the importance of adding Pietro Caselli to our hit list and emphasized his previous statement to us in Aruba that Caselli was crafty enough to try to take over as underboss to Vincenzo Cotillo.

We had already decided that Pietro Caselli had to be eliminated but when Nicolo maintained that his own group could perform this operation without our involvement we vetoed his suggestion very firmly.

I answered for our group by informing our ally, "Nicolo, when Pietro Caselli is rubbed out it is essential that you have a watertight alibi because the cops will make you their number one suspect.

When the killing is performed you must be highly visible in a public place where respectable citizens can testify to your presence.

All we will want from you and your friends is information on Pietro Caselli's customary movements. Then you can relax and forget about eliminating the opposition".

Nicolo accepted my suggestions, which in effect were instructions, with equanimity as he realized the common sense behind them.

He agreed to use his local knowledge and his men to discover Caselli's normal routine. It would mean covert surveillance for a few days and maybe even meeting the prospective victim personally to allow Nicolo to put on a non-aggressive posture in order to get a clue on the most suitable occasion to eliminate his opponent.

* * * * *

Nicolo soon discovered the required information. He phoned me and asked me to meet him promptly.

I was well aware that the fuzz would be keeping a tentative eye on Nicolo and I had no wish to be noticed by their beady eyes consorting with Nicolo at his home so we arranged to meet him and his wife 'accidentally' for next-day lunch at the Ristorante Palladia in downtown Montreal.

We had a seemingly innocent reason for being acquainted with Nicolo. He had, with our connivance, set up a phoney contract with our Pharos International company to check the books and recommend management improvements to the several pizza parlours and cafes owned by Nicolo's group.

All perfectly legal and, of course, we respectable directors of a large trading corporation had no idea of Nicolo's connection with organized crime!

However we, Firdaussi and I, eventually joined Nicolo and his spouse at their table in the Palladia.

Nicolo was quite jubilant at his success in getting the information which might well extinguish the hopes of his chief opponent.

We ordered aperitifs and over our drinks Nicolo explained, "I contacted Caselli and the two-faced bastard invited me to join him for a drink and conversation, not realizing that I had been informed that he was in cahoots with that fat pig Paolo to have me knocked off. I acted innocently and put on the pretense of wanting his inestimable business advice.

I guess he fell for it hook, line and sinker because he affably told me, among other unimportant snippets, of his addiction to movies and that he intended to see Godfather 2 at the Rio cinema next Friday evening.

Naturally I was elated at this bit of info. and soon withdrew from his company but not before exchanging mutual assurances of eternal co-operation!!"

Nicolo paused after his monologue and sipped his drink as he eyed me to see what effect this revelation would have.

I grinned and answered, " Nicolo, to thwart a two-faced bastard you had to be a two-faced bastard yourself. You did well and something can now be organized to take advantage of Caselli's probable movements next Friday, which is only three days away. It is feasible that something may prevent him visiting the Rio but we will take a chance on that.

Nicolo, your son Vittorio will be needed on this occasion in order to recognize Pietro Caselli as he did when Paolo Velio got hit. Is that OK by you?"

Nicolo nodded his assent so I continued, "In that case send him to our home on Thursday afternoon. He can stay the night with us and learn the proposed procedure. He will probably be driving a get-away car after the hit but I assure you both he will not be pulling a trigger."

At this remark a look of relief lit up Nicolo's wife's face and Nicolo himself agreed to ask Vittorio to visit us as suggested.

We then continued to enjoy our meal with never another word about the proposed mayhem or any other criminal project.

In some aspects we could be considered quite civilized!

CHAPTER FOURTEEN

GOODBYE PIETRO CASELLI

Vittorio turned up at our home on Thursday afternoon as instructed, in time to join us for dinner and drive us to the restaurant in my car. We again chose the Bridge restaurant about half way along the road to St. Jerome.

Our party, apart from Firdaussi, Vittorio, and me, included Angelo and his wife Maria.

Luigi had decided that Angelo and I were to be the shooters in the Caselli elimination so he left us to plan our tactics and discuss them with him next morning. So he and wife Tania went to dinner on their own in Montreal.

During our meal we put Vittorio in the picture about the part he was to play in the proposed killing. He was to pick up a hire car under an assumed name and drive us to the parking place nearest to the main doors of the Rio cinema.

We planned to arrive there in time to survey the arrival of the audience. Vittorio was to scrutinize the crowd until he recognized our target, Pietro Caselli.

Once we knew that Caselli had indeed turned up we would have a long and boring wait until the audience started pouring out through the cinema doors.

We decided to console ourselves during our sojourn by stacking up with cigarettes, chewing gum and a couple of sandwiches. Angie and I would each carry a snub-nosed .357 Smith and Wesson revolver, weapons supplied by Vittorio for the Paolo Velio killing and un-used for that job.

* * * * *

Luigi agreed with our proposed action so we found ourselves at the appointed time stuck in a suitable parking spot near the Rio cinema main entry, near enough to allow Vittorio to pick out

Pietro Caselli as he entered the cinema. There was, naturally, the chance that he would not turn up that evening.

However, he turned up as we hoped to Vittorio's excited,"There he is, there he is, that's him in the black overcoat!"

Angie and I had time to scrutinize the guy in the black overcoat before he vanished from sight through the glass doors.

After all, it's safer to identify your target before you shoot him. You don't want to kill the wrong guy, do you?

So we had our couple of hours wait; nearly smoked ourselves to death and chewed hot dogs chased by tins of Coke until we were fed up with the tastes of both.

As Angelo remarked with some sarcasm, "Why the hell didn't we buy tickets and see the show?"

I sat beside Vittorio, the driver, and Angie sat on the right hand side of the back seat. This allowed both of us to shoot out of our adjacent windows in comfort, each of us being right-handed.

The cans and other debris from our eating and smoking session were stored in a bag for later safe disposal. We had no wish to leave anything in the hire car that some hawk-eyed forensic snoop could link to us. Not even a finger print as we all wore thin plastic gloves from start to finish of our escapade.

* * * * *

We soldiered on in comparitive idleness until the first eager to leave members of the audience hurried out from the locked open glass doors of the Rio.

Then we were suddenly all agog as we anticipated the exit of Pietro Caselli.

The ensuing crowd ambled unhurriedly through the doors while we scanned every male for our target in the black overcoat.

I reckon we all three recognized Pietro simultaneously as he strolled out putting on his overcoat.

He ambled along the sidewalk as he leisurely buttoned up.

I hissed at Vittorio, "Take off, mister, slowly, and gradually overtake him."

We crawled along at walking pace while Pietro gradually left the thinning crowd. He was obviously going to pick up his parked car.

At the opportune moment I told Vittorio, "Get up alongside him, this is it!" Just as I said this Pietro turned off the sidewalk as if he intended to cross the street.

He was a sitting target, not more than two yards from his killers.

Angie and I fired immediately in unison. We fired three very rapid shots each and the magnum bullets all struck Pietro Caselli in the chest over the heart area. He couldn't have known what hit him it was so sudden and unexpected, he must have been dead before his knees buckled and his body slumped on the roadway.

" Let's go, Vittorio, and take it easy." I instructed our driver as he joined the traffic lane, "And drive up plenty of side streets to avoid sticking to the main stem, some bright witness might have noted our car registration number and we don't want a shoot-out with a snooping police patrol car!"

Both of us shooters had reloaded our magnum snubbies in case of trouble. Although we heard the cops' sirens shrieking as they raced en route to the killing zone we reached our planned spot where we ditched our hire car with no further problem.

Making sure that Vittorio removed our bag of debris we each strolled individually to our pick-up car parked in the next street.

It was there, as planned, with Firdaussi at the wheel and Maria, Angelo's spouse beside her. Firdy drove us steadily to the Ristorante Palladia where we ambled in as usual and joined Luigi and Tania, already seated at our customary table.

I gave a brief affirmative nod to Luigi to denote success in our venture and we then enjoyed an excellent dinner with no further mention of life and death mayhem.

In fact we didn't discuss the killing until we were safely home at my place. It was the age old mafia safeguard - Keep Your Mouth Shut!

* * * * *

CHAPTER FIFTEEN

GO FOR COCAINE

We had a long discussion on the feasibility of contacting the drug barons in Colombia to arrange a supply of cocaine to be distributed in North America and Europe.

At the same time giving the Colombian mobsters the opportunity to use our extensive money laundering facilities for a modest fee.

Concurrent with the discussion was the need to visit the brains of our organization, Otto Guynemer, at his noble residence, Cottingham Hall, in England.

Angelo and his wife Maria were more than pleased to stay in Canada and supervise our new members, Nicolo and Vittorio Rizzoli, as well as our narcotics shipments through Montreal. Duties for which they were more than capable of handling.

So Luigi and spouse Tania accompanied by Firdaussi and me took flight in the earliest aircraft which happened to be Lufthansa and, after a few tedious hours, arrived at London Heathrow International Airport.

Here, as usual, we were met by Fred Pierce, Otto Guynemer's head chauffeur, and ushered to a resplendent Rolls-Royce sedan.

Cottingham Hall never failed to impress us. It was a vast Tudor era residence beautifully situated in a very lush and large slice of English countryside. How Otto Guynemer managed to gain ownership of this veritable palace plus an accompanying fortune by virtue of a skilful marriage also never failed to impress us!

Otto greeted us with his customary *bonhomie* and led us into an anteroom for drinks and a brief pre-dinner general chat.

Our bags had been taken to our rooms by a hefty footman and a bevy of chamber-maids. Otto was never short of staff!

The superb meal and accompanying vintage wines were up to normal Cottingham Hall standards so, fully satiated, we were shepherded back to the anteroom, complete with crackling log fire, and settled down to business, a chore aided by endless drinks and clouds of expensive cheroot smoke.

Otto opened proceedings with, "We've been flooding North America and Europe with heroin and associated dope to our great financial advantage for years and there remains an adequate demand for our products. However, we are all aware that there is a growing requirement for cocaine and if we don't negotiate the lion's share of this market for our benefit, someone else will."

He concluded by asking, "What are your comments?"

I had just opened my mouth to reply when Luigi beat me to it by stating, "My comments are that we have to capture a substantial portion of this market and the main item we have to decide is where are we going to source the coke. What growers are we going to buy it from?"

There was a general mumble of agreement with Luigi's proposal as I added,"I agree with Luigi's comments absolutely and I am sure the ladies feel the same way."

I glanced at Firdaussi and Maria who nodded their affirmation. They nodded because they were both guzzling, with obvious enjoyment, a couple of large Bloody Marys!

The ball was back in Otto's court.

He carried on," I've been doing a lot of pondering on this subject and much detailed investigation of the possibilities which have arisen. I am suggesting strongly that we get our cocaine from South America by virtue of contact with one of the leading Colombian drug cartels."

He paused and looked around his audience, obviously expecting comments.

I now aired my Colombian knowledge mainly to let my bosses know I had pondered on the situation.

My brilliant exposition was,"The chief cartel at present is the Medellin organization who get their coke from Chile and other South American countries. I guess if we contact them we'll have to pay them in goddamned pesos!"

The last sally at least raised a few smiles.

Luigi grinned and interjected," And I guess they won't haggle with U.S. dollars, Deac.

You will soon find out, anyway, because you'll be the guy doing the negotiations!"

This remark caused all round chuckles and Firdaussi, having finished her current Bloody Mary, put her spoke in, " I look forward to a vacation in Colombia, wherever that is, but I want to know if there are any up-market hotels in Medellin. My slum living days were over long ago!"

Now it was Otto's turn again, he, with a laugh, said,"You have no need to worry about your standard of living, Firdy, because you will not be going to Colombia. You and Deac will be talking to their contact man in Miami, Florida, and we all know there are plenty of top hotels in Miami."

He paused for a drag at his cheroot, then continued with, "Colombia is too dangerous for us to visit at the present time, you and Deacon would probably get kidnapped and we'd have to bail you out with a huge ransom."

Otto grinned at me and added, "In pesos!"

So it was eventually agreed that Firdaussi and I would visit the Colombian agent in Miami to arrange a contract for a supply of street-ready cocaine to be shipped to Luigi in Sicily. This was really a test case because we needed to distribute coke in Europe through Sicily and Corsica then on to Marseilles and Paris, France, where we had set up an efficient organization years before.*

If we left it to the Medellin cartel to ship our narcotics to Canada via Mexico and U.S.A. it would be a very expensive operation considering all the necessary bribery and corruption hand-outs involved.

We preferred to control our shipments from start to finish.
It proved cheaper in the long run. And safer.

Otto emphasized that we must contact Santos Salvatore before starting our business in Miami. Santos was the headman of Cosa Nostra who we knew more than well as he was the guy who initiated our big hit on JFK in Dallas, 1963.

Otto, foreseeing the outcome of our meeting, (as usual!),had already contacted Santos who was only too glad to help as, in any case, the Medellin cartel agent had to have Santos' permission to operate in Florida and our introduction would be simplified.

Plus, Santos Salvatore, as mafia Don, knew he would receive a suitable monetary appreciation of his services to our Sicilian cartel. After all, business is business!

* * * * *

* See "The Cairo Connection" Chapter 20, p.201

CHAPTER SIXTEEN

THE COLOMBIA CONNECTION

I returned to Montreal together with Firdy as we wanted to see how Angelo and his wife had coped during our absence. Also to put them in the picture concerning our projected plan to contact the Colombian drug cartel for the supply of cocaine.

There had been no major problems with our re-organized drug racket in Canada as Angie was a very experienced and capable mobster who would have sorted out any administrative trouble efficiently.

After a day or two getting in touch with our new colleagues Nicolo Rizzoli and his son Vittorio who were still grateful to our clique for forcibly removing their adversaries thus assuring Nicolo's leadership of Cosa Nostra in Canada, we bade adieu to Angie and Maria yet again and made for Florida.

We struggled our way through Immigration and Customs at Miami International Airport, rang Santos Salvatore to inform him of our arrival, paid our couple of bucks toll money to the hefty Afro-Americans who man-handled our baggage cart for the last ten yards to the exit and hailed a taxi.

Our cabby was not the brightest of guys but we eventually reached the address given us by Santos Salvatore.

We guessed this was Salvatore's chief residence in Miami. It was a large up-market house in a treed lot which allowed plenty of privacy. The large iron gates opened automatically to allow our cab to enter, operated by a guy in a small guardhouse.

The driveway was curved, making the house invisible from the road. Santos Salvatore was standing in front of the door waiting to greet us. He had obviously been informed of our arrival by the guy in the guardhouse.

We were greeted by Don Santos very affably with a hearty handshake for me and a courteous kiss for Firdaussi.

I remembered that Santos was a Cosa Nostra don of the old school and took care to bow my head respectfully after he shook my hand. He was traditional Sicilian mafioso and expected some sign of respect from visitors.

However, after the initial greeting was over he addressed me as Deacon and Firdy as Firdaussi. Then to my astonishment he told us to call him by his first name, Santos!

This really was familiarity to the point of intimacy!

He obviously considered us as business equals at least.

Remember also that he was well aware that our immediate boss, Luigi Ferraro, was head of a powerful Sicilian mafia family of which Firdaussi and I were long time associates. On top of that salient fact was our group contained a bunch of highly skilled professional assassins who had performed the execution of JFK under his initial guidance.

To put it briefly, Santos Salvatore wanted to maintain his close relationship with the Good Ol' Boys!

* * * * *

After an amiable discussion with Santos, well supplied with our favorite drinks, he informed us that he would arrange our meeting with the Colombian agent, a guy named Roderigo Sanchez, and would contact us at our hotel to tell us the time and place for the rendezvous.

Santos was well aware that the heroin which drifted down to his outfit in Florida was supplied by our shipments through Montreal, Canada, via the Bonnano crime family in New York.

So, although he was getting a supply of cocaine from Colombia via Mexico, he mentioned that he could easily switch to our cocaine from Canada when the time came, "If the price is right!"

Firdy and I left Santos in good humor and headed for the Berkeley hotel in down-town Miami, looking forward to a good lunch as usual.

We booked in to the best suite in the house, remembered to ring Santos with our 'phone number and ordered our grub.

Life was a perpetual holiday to Firdy and me even though we were working for the mob!

* * * * *

Santos soon told us where to meet the Colombian drug guy. It was a private address in Miami and the time of meeting was "as soon as possible"!

So we called a cab and reached the address within fifteen minutes.

It was a modest house but we noticed a couple of expensive looking cars in the driveway. A Jaguar and a Mercedes.

We ambled to the front door and I thumbed the bell-push.

A short delay during which we knew we were being scanned through a small glass eye-piece in the door frame.

The door opened and a shortish, squat guy surveyed us unsmilingly.

"Who are you?", he queried in heavily accented English.

I told him who we were and mentioned that we hoped he was expecting us.

"Santos said you were coming", he replied, "Come in."

He led us down a short corridor where we noticed a hard-faced guy standing on the alert. Roderigo made a nodding motion and the hood vanished round the back. There was no effort made to introduce us to this tough so we surmised he was a resident bodyguard.

We were shown into a decently furnished living-room and asked to seat ourselves in a couple of convenient armchairs.

Roderigo sat opposite and asked us bluntly what we wanted.

I responded by asking just as bluntly, "Tell us who you work for, Roderigo, and if we are happy with that we'll let you know what we want."

We could tell that Roderigo was a bit taken back by my rapid request. I wanted him to realise that we were doing him a favor, not vice versa. After all there were more ways to get cocaine than by using his contacts.

He started with, "I work for Pablo Escobar-Gavira,boss of our Medellin operation, and I have his authority to engage in any business arrangement which will prove beneficial to our cartel."

He paused and looked at me quizzically, obviously wondering if I was satisfied with his explanation.

I was more than impressed at his mention of Pablo Escobar-Gavira. This guy was one of the most violent killers in the business who had no compunction about fatally removing members of the Colombian police and judiciary who got in his way. A guy to watch very carefully if personal involvement was contemplated.

However, I told Roderigo that we were interested in purchasing large quantities of cocaine from his cartel for cash payment in American dollars, 25% in advance to show goodwill and the remaining 75% on receipt of the dope in Miami or wherever was most convenient in USA.

Roderigo, naturally, was inquisitive about who Firdy and I represented.

I mentioned we were a powerful Cosa Nostra family vouched for by the local mafia Don Santos Salvatore, emphasizing that I did not intend to give any names or personal details of our cartel members.

I finished with,"We will give you an order immediately for a substantial dope shipment on a trial basis. Give us a price for this trial shipment and you will be handed your 25%. On receipt of this shipment we will test for quality and when found satisfactory you will receive the remaining 75%. How does that suit you, Roderigo?"

Roderigo answered, "That suits me fine. Give me a 'phone number so that I can call you when I have organized your first order. Then we can meet again and you can hand over the goodwill cash."

I gave him our hotel number, we shook hands and he offered to run us back to our hotel rather than hire a cab.

We accepted and he personally drove us back to the Berkeley Hotel where he accepted our invitation to join us for lunch.

* * * * *

CHAPTER SEVENTEEN

ORGANIZATION AND METHOD

Before we had heard fom the Colombian cartel that our first cocaine order was ready for delivery we had, as a group, been considering a more sophisticated and secure method of running our narcotics shipments over the Canada/USA border.

Our current methods paid off but, on occasion, a load would be detected by the authorities and annexed.

This occasional loss we put down to business expenses but, each time, there was some danger that officialdom would follow up their temporary success and covertly learn a bit more about the organizers and the organizers being us, the Good Ol' Boys,we had no wish to be listed as Bad Boys on international police records!

So, in our wisdom, we had pondered on practical alternative methods of smuggling our goods over the border.

* * * * *

As my devoted readers will know our cartel had for years been using helicopters and light aircraft to deliver our drug shipments from Corsica to Marseilles, France.*

So, after much discussion with our bosses and other relevant mob members we hatched up a scheme involving surreptitious air flights trans-border. Naturally Firdaussi and I were ordered to organize and test the system, an obvious corollary as I was a qualified pilot. Ordered in a nice way, of course!

As usual we left Angie and his wife Maria to supervise affairs in Montreal and Firdy and I set off for Vancouver, way over on the west side of Canada.

* See "The Cairo Connection" page 269

We had already arranged to purchase a light helicopter from our old friend and accomplice Gerard Fenlac.

Gerard owned an aviation and air charter company near Paris, France and had played his part in organizing our get-away after the bloody Paris Massacre as the media called it.

The helicopter was purchased quite legally by our Pharos International Corporation branch in Montreal, Canada and was shipped to that city by our ocean-going tramp steamer which, incidentally, also carried our regular cargo of narcotics.

Pasquale Mangano, our trusted helicopter pilot in Corsica,had been instructed to meet us in Vancouver. Pasquale had been our get-away pilot after the Paris shooting, flying a machine ostensibly "stolen" from Gerard Fenlac's air charter company.

* * * * *

Firdy and I flew to Vancouver and had our Cadillac sedan shipped across Canada by rail-freight. We had no wish to drive about two and half thousand miles and were beginning to realise we were living in a mighty big country!

We booked in at the Columbia Carlton Hotel and ordered a room for Pasquale Mangano who we met at the International Airport just in time for him to join us for dinner.

He was put in the picture concerning our proposal to run illegal drug shipments across the Canada-USA border and agreed with us that he should take steps to register in both countries as an officially certified helicopter pilot.

With his extensive past experience this should not be difficult and, luckily, he had no criminal record with the French authorities; a claim which would certainly be checked by the Canadian and USA aviation authorities.

To further these requirements the three of us drove south to Bellingham, Washington State, USA, crossing the border at the Peace Arch crossing, the most convenient one en route from Vancouver.

At Bellingham our colleague Pasquale filled in the required paper work and had a short interview with a man from the aviation authority which Firdy and I attended as part-time interpreters. Pasquale's English was a bit stilted because he rarely used the language, normally speaking French or Italian back home in Corsica.

However, all went well and Pasquale was informed he would probably receive the official OK to his application in two or three weeks.

We took the opportunity to drive on to Seattle, the capital of Washington State, where we enjoyed some good food and bought many maps covering Washington and the neighboring state of Oregon.

Not being in a hurry we booked in for one night at the Grand Pacific Hotel and returned cross-border to Vancouver next day.

Back in Canada we went with Pasquale to the aviation authority to get him registered officially as a qualified helicopter pilot. As in USA he was told, after a short interview, that he would receive his papers in a couple of weeks.

Meanwhile we had to ship our new helicopter over to British Columbia. It was still crated dockside in Montreal.

We contacted our colleague, Angelo Rizzoli, who was supervising our cartel's interests and lived in Montreal, asking him to arrange the movement of the helicopter to the airport and get it assembled ready to take the air.

Pasquale had agreed to return to Montreal once his pilot registration had been finalized and test fly our machine. Then he intended to fly it in stages, from airport to airport across Canada to British Columbia.

In the meantime we had to organize a suitable landing area where we could base our helicopter. An area where constant take-offs and landings would not arouse suspicion.

By a bit of luck Pasquale Mangano had been looking for short term rental accommodation. At the realtor's office he had noticed a restaurant for sale at Harrison Hot Springs, a resort with many thermal springs and many visitors staying to enjoy the warm water. Somewhat to his surprise the realtor's listing noted "property includes registered helicopter landing and take-off zone".

He hastened to inform me of this rather singular circumstance and I wasted no time in following it up.

Pasquale, Firdy and I approached the realtor and soon found ourselves at Harrison Hot Springs, which is about fifty-five miles east of Vancouver and about twenty miles north of the Canada/USA border.

Here we discovered that the Acqua Caldo restaurant was an up-market joint, where if a customer asked the price he was soon told he couldn't afford to eat there!

The realtor showed us over the property, including the helicopter landing area which was concealed from public view by a thick growth of large trees and was associated with a useful hangar and a large workshop.

We were introduced to the owner, an elderly French guy, who was selling reluctantly due to complicated family and health problems.

The three of us, me, Firdaussi and Pasquale had a private pow-wow and finished up agreeing that this property would fit into our nefarious plans perfectly.

So, over a delicious dinner, I informed the realtor, a lady, that we would purchase the property if the financial records were checked by an accountant and found viable plus a satisfactory report from a qualified house inspector. If all appeared OK we would pay the asked price.

We returned to Vancouver driven by an elated realtor and were dropped off at our hotel.

Next morning I contacted Angelo in Montreal and told him to tell Niccolo Rizzoli, the Cosa Nostra boss who was controlled by our cartel, to find a French speaking guy in his mob who would be bright enough to manage our new acquisition, the Acqua Caldo restaurant.

I knew Nicolo owned several pizzeria restaurants in Quebec and one of his cronies who had managed one of them for several years was approached by Nicolo and asked if he would like to move to British Columbia.

This guy, Joseph Profaci, a long-time mobster and mafioso saw there might be some good pickings in this proposed job and said he would be keen to have a go if his wife was included.

She was included as requested and, of course, both being inhabitants in Quebec for many years they could speak French without hesitation.

So Mr. and Mrs. Profaci joined us in Vancouver, were told of our intentions and visited Acqua Caldo several times to get the feel of the place. The restaurant had excellent living accommodation on the upper floor which was an added bonus for our newcomers.

* * * * *

The completion of the Acqua Caldo sale just about coincided with the receipt of Pasquale's helicopter pilot registration papers both American and Canadian.

So off went Pasquale to Montreal to test fly our new helicopter and then return with it to our restaurant landing patch where it would be housed in the hangar.

At about the same time I had a message from Angelo who was supervising our affairs in eastern Canada.

He had been informed by Santos Salvatore, the Cosa Nostra boss in Miami that our first cocaine order from Colombia had been delivered and awaited collection.

This meant a trip to Miami for Firdy and me to check and pay for the narcotics. The payment method had been agreed with Roderigo Sanchez the agent for the Colombian drug cartel. We had arranged to transfer the required funds from one of our banks accounts in Liechtenstein direct to another bank account in Liechtenstein owned by none other than Pablo Escobar-Gavira, murderous boss of the cocaine cartel. Even this feared killer was wise enough to organize a bank in Liechtenstein!

Our first visit in Miami was to our old chum Don Santos Salvatore. We took him and two bodyguards to a swell dinner at a restaurant of his choice. The bodyguards sat at a near-by table as our discussion with the Don was more than private.

Santos told us that he had arranged the testing and quantity checking of our shipment and it had passed muster.

Between mouthfuls he said, " Deacon, I want some of that dope, what's the price?"

Also between mouthfuls I answered, " Santos, to an old friend it's free, gratis and for nothing! You've done a lot for us on this deal and we'd like to show our appreciation."

This pleased Santos who responded with, " The dope is in a safe place and when you tell me where in USA you want it I will arrange transport. So all you guys have to do is contact Roderigo

Sanchez and go back to Canada."

So our dinner ended in good humor and affability. Next day we confirmed our payment to Roderigo Sanchez and flew back to Vancouver.

* * * * *

We were met by Pasquale Mangano who had already ensconced our helicopter in the hangar at Harrison Hot Springs.

Our next move was to contact the boss of the motorcycle gangsters in British Columbia and the adjoining Washington State in USA. This guy lived in Vancouver and had organized the Bikers, as his toughs were nicknamed, into a drug running mob.

These people rode powerful Harley Davidson motorbikes for pleasure and business and had made a significant contribution to organized crime in western Canada.

We arranged to meet the boss of the Bikers, an American named Dwain Jackson, whose level of business could in no way be considered impressive when compared to our cartel's world wide activity.

However he turned up at our Acqua Caldo restaurant in an expensive Gucci suit and the latest Mercedes convertible so he must have organized his rackets pretty efficiently.

We had our initial discussion upstairs in Joseph Profaci's apartment. Our requirements were explained.

Basically we needed Bikers to find or clear remote areas in the forests of Washington where our helicopter could land safely and take on a load of cocaine free from observation by law enforcement agencies. The helicopter would then snoop back over the USA/Canadian border and head for our site at Harrison Hot Springs to unload the dope ready for further distribution.

Dwain Jackson was impressed and stated his eagerness to proceed. We dropped a few hints about confidentiality and what would happen to Bikers or associates who blabbed.

Dwain had been a racketeer long enough to be well aware of the nasty fates suffered by opponents of the Sicilian Cosa Nostra. And we were Sicilian Cosa Nostra!

* * * * *

CHAPTER EIGHTEEN

DRUGS BY AIR

To check our new aviation scheme we arranged for Santos Salvatore to send our shipment of cocaine to Washington State where it was cached by Bikers under the control of Dwain Jackson.

Pasquale Mangano flew me down to Seattle, the capital of Washington because I wanted to supervise the chosing of a remote forest clearance area suitable for landing the helicopter and loading it with dope.

We left our helicopter at Seattle airport, met Dwain Jackson and decided on the location of our illegal landing spot. Then Jackson introduced us to his Biker crew, a hardy bunch of thugs, and we had a long, tedious drive to our proposed forest area.

It certainly was remote and the area didn't require much clearance to allow a safe landing and take-off according to the practiced opinion of Pasquale Mangano.

So we returned to Seattle and arranged to make our first smuggling run in three days time. Dwain Jackson was to stay in USA while Pasquale and I flew our helicopter back to Harrison Hot Springs in British Columbia.

* * * * *

The initial pick-up of dope went flawlessly.
Dwain Jackson directed his Biker crew to transport the load to our selected forest clearing in a couple of trucks.

Pasquale Mangano and I gave the truck crew sufficient time to reach the clearing then took off and soon reached our position. We flew very low and circled once before receiving the OK signal from the ground.

Pasquale touched down with no problem, even though the clearing was intentionally confined, and the ground crew, under my direction, soon transferred the packed narcotics from trucks to helicopter.

On the rapid completion of this task I rejoined Pasquale in the helicopter which immediately took off and headed north to the Canadian border.

Our tactic, to aid security and to try to avoid visual recognition from the ground was to climb to our service ceiling and cross the border at a great height.

Luckily we did not need to stay at that altitude for long as it was more than chilly. We aimed for Harrison Hot Springs and descended fast.

On landing at our private helicopter base we soon had the machine, with the shipment of cocaine included, snugly hidden in our hangar. Here the dope rested for a couple of days until Dwain Jackson arrived with a select crew of his Bikers.

They arrived individually in several large and expensive sedans, giving the impression that they were visiting to enjoy lunch at our up-market Acqua Caldo restaurant.

They did this with gusto but wasted little time, after quaffing their brandies and coffee, in craftily driving over to our forest-concealed hangar and transferring the cocaine to their automobiles.

We considered this technique caused less casual attention from other visitors than driving up in noisy trucks manned by a bunch of blue-collar worhmen obviously engaged on a transport operation.

As our boss, mafia Don Luigi Ferraro, insisted, "Reduce the risk!"

When the dope had been placed in the cars they drifted off individually leaving Dwain Jackson with us to discuss the methods of distribution in British Columbia, the larger proportion being sent across Canada to our base in Montreal.

Dwain, of course, wanted to ensure he was getting his own substantial cut of the proceeds! After all, he also had a tough bunch of Bikers who weren't intending to work for nothing!

* * * * *

CHAPTER NINETEEN

TEMPUS FUGIT

Our Cosa Nostra cartel seemed to be perfectly balanced and organized to optimum efficiency after many strenuous and dangerous years of hard slog.

Things had not always gone smoothly as we built up the system but we had adapted, altered and modified various aspects to the best of our ability.

We had bribed, terrified or coerced scores of susceptible politicians, officials and lawmen to aid our illicit skullduggery and found that money could solve most problems. If money did not work the bullet or bomb always assisted us to get our chosen results.

So our mob members were all seriously wealthy. However they were all getting seriously older!!

Firdaussy and I well remember the date when our mafia Don, Luigi, phoned us from Sicily with a real bit of bad news.

The date was 1st. June, 1983 when Luigi told us that Otto Guynemer was dead. Otto had long been the big brain behind our organization and had just reached his ninetieth year of age.

However, he had not died of natural causes. It shook us to hear that his butler had found him shot to death at his magnificent residence in England, Cottingham Hall.

As Luigi stated in his own inimitable style, "Some bastards have knocked off Otto. Who in the name of hell could have done that?

Get over there , Deac, and check what the local cops are doing and thinking. Put on the dear old friend and fellow director act. We gotta know whose behind this killing, Deac, they may well be after all of us!

Get over there, pronto, and send for me when you've got a clue as to what's going on."

Firdaussi and I were in Montreal, Canada, when the news hit us. We had returned from British Columbia after setting up the helicopter system for smuggling cocaine into Canada and using the same means to ship marijuana from British Columbia to the United States.

We passed the news of Otto's demise to Angelo and Maria, adding that Luigi had instructed Firdy and me to head for England to discover more about the shooting and what the police were up to.

Angelo and his spouse wished us luck in our quest and emphasized their willingness to join us if required.

So Firdy and I soon found ourselves in an Air Canada flight heading for Heathrow Airport, England.

* * * * *

Luigi had already phoned Cottingham Hall, spoken to Otto's old chauffeur Fred Pierce and told him our expected time of arrival at Heathrow Airport.

So, at the appointed time Fred was there, as so often before, ready to drive us to Cottingham Hall in one of Otto's Rolls-Royce limousines.

Fred, naturally enough, was greatly upset at the unexpected murder of his boss. Apart from an uncertain future he had to suffer seemingly endless interrogation by detectives from the Criminal Investigation Department of the East Sussex Constabulary led by a hawk like Chief Inspector Gates.

Fred Pierce was not a happy man but he transported us to Cottingham Hall without problem.

The first person we met was the long established butler who recognized us immediately as intimate friends of his dead boss Otto Guynemer.

He was another unhappy man and rather dolefully asked, "Will you be staying, Sir, Madam?"

I rapidly explained that we could not stay as we had not been invited by the owner because he was unexpectedly dead. We would stay at the nearest decent hostelry if he, the butler, would recommend one.

In the meantime we wished to meet the senior police officer present and introduce ourselves. We guessed there were detectives snooping around because there was a uniformed cop stationed at the main door in addition to a couple of police vehicles.

Fred Pierce the chauffeur suggested we should leave our baggage in the Rolls-Royce and he would run us to our hotel after we had finished with the police.

That suited us so Firdaussi and I ambled up to the cop on the door, explained briefly that we were old friends of Otto Guynemer and wished to speak to the senior officer present.

The cop nodded his understanding of our request and asked us to follow him.

We pursued the cop at regulation police marching speed until we reached a familiar anteroom. He waved us to a halt and entered the room returning shortly with a middle-aged guy in civilian clothes.

The cop retired to his place of duty and the civilian eyed us closely and introduced himself, " Good afternoon, I am Chief Inspector Gates of the local Criminal Investigation Department, Sussex Constabulary, looking into this unfortunate occurrence to Mr. Otto Guynemer. I understand you are old friends of the deceased gentleman?"

I acknowledged our relationship to Otto Guynemer and, in my turn, introduced ourselves.

Gates offered his hand to us both and asked, "You have arrived at an opportune time, would it be convenient for you both to have a chat with me and my sergeant in private?"

This chief dick was not wasting any time.

I agreed we would "have a chat", knowing full well that this was going to be the start of a lengthy interrogation.

Gates called into the anteroom for his sergeant, led us into the library and asked us to be seated. The sergeant joined us and was introduced as Detective-Sergeant Philips. He sat at the table notebook at the ready. Then he asked us, "Would you give me your full names and home address, please?"

I glanced at Gates who nodded his assent, so we did as the sergeant requested and gave him our Canadian address with our full names. He thanked us on completion of this, to him, routine business.

Then Chief Inspector Gates took over and addressed me with, "How long have you known Mr. Guynemer, Mr. Roy?"

"About forty-six years", I replied after a rapid calculation.

"Would you mind telling me the circumstances of how and where you first met him?", continued Gates.

"I met him in Cairo, Egypt, when he offered me a job", I responded,

"That's a faraway city, Mr. Roy, may I ask what you were doing in Cairo prior to meeting Mr. Guynemer?"

"You may ask, Inspector", I paused briefly to let him know that I knew I did not have to answer, then I went on, "I was in the Royal Air Force as a corporal armorer and by sheer chance Mr. Guynemer learned I was the son of an old friend of his who had been killed in World War One. I guess mainly on emotional impulse he eventually offered me a job in the commercial company where he was president and owner."

Gates thanked me for the information and turned to Firdaussi. "Mrs. Roy, would you be kind enough to tell me how you first met Mr. Otto Guynemer."

Firdaussi lied brazenly and coolly, just like her husband, as she stated, " I met him through my husband when I was introduced to Mr. Guynemer at a social function in Cairo."

I mean to say, Firdy could not tell Gates that she was a prostitute in a brothel controlled by Guynemer's mafia cartel, could she?

Gates thanked Firdy for her obviously frank answer and queried, "Mr.Roy, have you any knowledge Mr. Guynemer had enemies violent enough to murder him?"

I put on a slightly shocked expression as I emphasized, " Never could I imagine that situation, Mr. Guynemer was a very friendly person and helped people willingly rather than make enemies of them. Surely, Inspector, this dreadful deed was performed by someone intending robbery?"

Firdy echoed my statement by simulating wide-eyed surprise that dear old Otto Guynemer should have vicious enemies.

After all, he had only organized a couple dozen serious massacres during his hectic career, how could he have nasty enemies?!

However, Chief Inspector Gates knew nothing of Otto Guynemer's checkered career and no member of our mob was likely to tell him.

Gates was aware from long experience that Firdy and I were getting fed up with interrogation so he thanked us politely for our co-operation, asked us to keep in touch during the rest of our visit and escorted us to the door where chauffeur Fred Pierce was waiting patiently to drive us to our hotel. He shook our hands and we parted amiably.

* * * * *

We stayed on in England for about a fortnight and suffered a couple more interrogation sessions with the law during which we gave nothing important away.

In fact we took care not to elaborate when we answered Gates' questions. It is surprising what a smart cop can infer from an unguarded response.

We contacted the head office of the Pharos International Corporation in London and ascertained the address and 'phone number of Otto Guynemer's personal attorney-at-law. This was not difficult because Firdy and I were not only directors but part-owners of the company as were the other senior mob members.

This lawyer told us he had Otto Guynemer's will and last testament and would communicate with us if, after scrutiny, there was anything in it "to our advantage." We also asked this professional gentleman to contact a suitable funeral director in order to get Otto put away decently. Otto, to our knowledge, wished to be cremated so we included this information in our request and asked to be told about the arrangements so we could attend and pay Otto our last respects.

After this bit of business was accomplished we flew back to our home in Montreal, Canada and reported by 'phone immediately to our boss, Luigi Ferraro, in Sicily. He was pleased with our contacts to police and lawyer but was still concerned about not knowing who had killed Otto Guynemer.

Angelo and Maria had stayed in Montreal during our visit to England and, naturally enough, were eager to know the results of our visit. We took them out to dine at our favorite Ristorante Palladia and put them in the picture.

Nearly a month passed while we checked our USA and Canada drug, vice and associated rackets until we had word from Guynemer's lawyer. He asked us to visit his office in London as he must read the will to the beneficiaries according to custom. At the same time we could attend Otto Guynemer's funeral service, somewhat delayed due to police reluctance to release the body.

Both dates were two weeks away so I hastily informed Luigi in Sicily, Angelo Rizzoli and spouse Maria our colleagues in Montreal and our old buddy in Cairo, Egypt, Abdul Mahmoud.

* * * * *

Angelo, Maria, Firdaussi and I took off for London three days later after ascertaining that both Luigi and Abdul Mahmoud would be joining us with their respective wives.

On arrival we took a cab to the Grand Imperial Hotel and, to the gratification of reception and management, booked all four of their available suites before settling in and enjoying a very good dinner.

We met Luigi and Tania at Heathrow International Airport the next morning, settled them in their private suite; had lunch together and straight away left for Heathrow, yet again, to meet Abdul and his wife Chantal.

As we hadn't seen Abdul for a number of years and I, for one, had never met his wife, our rendezvous was somewhat tumultuous. However, before it reached the disorderly stage we called a couple cabs and headed for the Grand Imperial.

Abdul and Chantal were soon settled comfortably in their up-market suite, which they both appreciated.

We all bundled in here with the new arrivals as we had much to talk about. After booking dinner we ordered room service to supply us with ample drinks to oil our vocal chords.

We formed two natural groups. The four ladies in the bedroom, plotting how to spend a small fortune on the latest London fashions. The men in the reception room discussing past, present and future activity.

A major topic was Otto Guynemer's will. What intriguing details would be disclosed when we all attended his lawyer's office the day after tomorrow? As each of us had amassed large quantities of criminally earned pelf during the past several decades nobody was very worried whether or not Otto had bequeathed him anything. However it was interesting to conjecture.

There was also the matter of the legal money cached in a Swiss bank since the end of World War Two. This amounted to over twenty million US dollars when it was deposited, most of it from the sale of our North Delta Trading Corporation in Egypt. The deposit had been registered in our names, the leading mobsters. Any three of us could sign checks to draw cash to cover emergencies which might arise.

No checks had ever been issued so that large sum, plus interest, was available to us if we so decided.

There was also the question of Pharos International Corporation. This was a flourishing company registered in London but operating world-wide. We were all directors and virtual owners of this organization. What to do with it now that the president, Otto Guynemer was gone for ever? He was the brains and organizer behind it.

We chatted on and on about this and that until dinner time when we all trooped down to the dining room and enjoyed a long and tasty meal together.

After the almost statutory coffees and brandies: which I was pleased to see Abdul knocking back regardless of his Moslem faith; we decided to call it a day and all re-trooped back to our suites, after deciding that we would spend the next day viewing the sights of London.

Firdy and I slept the sleep of the just as I am sure did all our colleagues.

* * * * *

We reached the lawyer's office in good time as he suggested reading Otto Guynemer's last will and testament at 11 am.

His receptionist led us into the so-called "reading room".

This was comfortably furnished with ample seating and a convenient table.

The lawyer entered with a clerk, welcomed us and asked us to give our names to the clerk, which we all did. The lawyer sat at the table replete with numerous documents.

Otto left just about all his property and wealth to his old colleagues. His estate at Cottingham Hall went to all of us equally "to be used and dealt with as we decided after consultation".

His private bank accounts with millions of pounds sterling and US dollars deposited in banks world-wide were to be allocated to us in equal shares. There were no other investments which surprised us because we knew for sure that he had purchased stocks and shares in the past. He had obviously sold his investments to avoid financial complications.

There were two codicils which the lawyer suggested were more advisory than legal.

One was that we should sell our company, Pharos International Corporation and put the proceeds in a trust to be organized "for the benefit of mankind". Was Otto's conscience pricking him?!

The other was that we should empty our legal Swiss bank account and split the proceeds equally.

The final touch was an individual sealed letter to each of us. On reading these personal messages from Otto we were intrigued to discover his thanks for our "long co-operation" and a suggestion to "retire from business" and enjoy the remainder of our lives in peace. To retire from business meant quitting the rackets, not an easy matter for a Cosa Nostra cartel led by Don Luigi Ferraro who was still in business in Sicily.

* * * * *

CHAPTER TWENTY

FINALE

Before we dispersed after hearing the reading of Otto Guynemer's last will and testament we had a long discussion concerning our future actions with regard to the joint bequests which Otto had left to us mob leaders.

Luigi, our new overall boss pointed out that as we were Cosa Nostra there was no question of individual retirement as suggested in the will. As Luigi had told me forcibly many years ago " Once you are in you are in forever". Of course, this was traditional mafia custom.

So, with some reluctance, we agreed to press on with the rackets until we dropped dead or were too old to move!

Luigi and the rest of us were still worried at not knowing who had whacked Otto Guynemer. Was some group going to knock us off one by one? And who the hell could they be? It is very difficult to protect yourself against an unknown assailant.

Anyway Luigi, wife Tania, Angelo and Maria departed for Sicily and business while Ferdaussi, Abdul and wife Chantal and me elected to stay at Cottingham Hall, the ancient estate which was now joint mob property.

This was a great relief for the butler, Fred Pierce the chauffeur and the other staff to learn they were not going to be fired.

Abdul and Chantal told us they needed a holiday away from the Middle East and their two sons, who were educated and living in England, could join them at Cottingham Hall and taste the fruits of gracious living.

We agreed with them wholeheartedly and told them to keep in touch because Firdy and I were returning to Montreal to check how our Cosa Nostra system was progressing.

* * * * *

Our first task in Montreal was to make ourselves comfortable in our very up-market home. Our second task was to contact

Nicolo Rizzoli and invite him and spouse Giuseppa to dine with us at our favorite Ristorante Palladia. We wished to put Nicolo, our top man in Canada, in the picture concerning Otto Guynemer's abrupt demise and how that affected our criminal cartel. Of course, we did not intend to disclose anything about Otto's bequests.

Nicolo was in good form and appeared to have everything under control but he did emphasize that a certain element in the New York Bonnano family seemed to be interfering with the normal good relationship between New York and Montreal. Nothing serious as yet but the situation would need watching.

The mafia Bonnano family were of prime influence in our drug transmission and distribution system.

Nicolo told us that his son Vittorio was a chip off the old block and was rapidly becoming a major organizer in the system.

This pleased us as Vittorio had worked with us on certain sanguinary matters locally and performed as expected. He was obviously well on his way to becoming a Good Ol' Boy!

So after an excellent and prolonged meal we parted from our guests very affably and retired to our homes. It had been a mutually informative session.

* * * * *

Luigi and party had flown back to their manor in Sicily after learning about Otto Guynemer's bequests.

Luigi's only son was his heir and successor as Don of the Ferraro mafia family and naturally he had been in control during Luigi's absence.

Luigi and Angelo with their spouses were met at Syracuse by one of their "soldiers" and driven to their manor at high speed.

There had been a resurgence of the Corleoni clan since their leaders had been decimated by us in the Marieno massacre.

They were, yet again, taking over or wiping out mafia families in Sicily and annexing a large percentage of the profits from the businesses operated by those families.

The Corleoni were, very unusually, poking their noses into the Ferraro family area in eastern Sicily. This did not please the ebullient Luigi so he sent a stern message to the Corleoni clan.

This rather forceful missive implied that if the Corleoni faction persisted in poking their evil snouts into Ferraro territory they would certainly get their pig-like heads shot off in the traditional mafia fashion!

Such an emphatic response really upset the Corleoni who considered they were the power centre of the mafia so they applied to the Cosa Nostra Commission for permission to murder Luigi Ferraro. As they controlled the Commission they soon got the OK to knock off Luigi.

As we know, the Commission was originally inaugurated by all the leading mafia families in Sicily to reduce the mayhem between rival coteries when disputes occurred. The Commission met in conclave to assess complaints and negotiate reasonable solutions. They could also authorize the final solution, death, if no other answer seemed feasible.

Luigi and his cohorts soon heard about the Corleoni skullduggery and Luigi, in his usual fashion, decided that attack was preferable to defense.

Now Otto Guynemer had departed there was no other colleague available, with such vast experience, to suggest the most suitable means of attack in the circumstances.

So Luigi, rather impetuously, mounted his numerous "soldiers" in suitable trucks and automobiles, heavily armed, and headed straight for the commune of Corleone which is in the Palermo province, population then about ten thousand and roughly one hundred miles from Luigi's manor.

Luigi intended to cause an uproar in the Corleoni clan home town plus slaughtering as many of their leaders and "soldiers" as possible. This, he guessed, would put them off gunning for Luigi and his cohorts for a long time.

At least he had the advantage of surprise. Nobody other than an experienced assassin like Luigi would dare to attack the dreaded Corleoni gang on their home territory.

Of course Angelo Rizzoli was number two man to Luigi and it will be remembered that he also had taken part in many successful gun battles and summary executions including firing the first shot in the JFK assassination in Dallas, Texas. So the invading force was led by a redoubtable pair of hitmen.

Luigi's mobile battle squad rumbled into Corleone and Luigi, in the leading automobile, stopped outside a bar, entered and at gunpoint dragged out a fat guy who was obviously the boss.

With the Colt .45 pistol muzzle stuck forcibly in the quivering tub of lard's left ear-hole Luigi snarled, "Where's the Don live?"

"Up there, up there!" blurted the panic stricken bar-keeper, pointing up the road, "In those big gates, that's where he lives!"

Luigi turned his head and shouted to the following vehicle, an automobile holding five "soldiers" , "Go in there", indicating the bar, "and knock off every bastard you see moving!"

As his men leapt out of the vehicle to obey his order Luigi squeezed the trigger of his Colt automatic and released his hold on the fat man, allowing the corpse to drop untidily on the sidewalk.

Luigi hastily re-entered the leading car and tore up the road to the big gates, followed by the rest of his vengeful army of gunmen.

The gates, fortunately, were wide open probably due to the local feeling that nobody in his right senses would attack the dreaded Corleoni mob in their home town. How wrong they were!

There was one guard on duty who ambled out of the guard house and waved the lead car down. That was his last official action because Angelo Rizzoli, in the rear passenger seat, shot him down with a short burst from his Uzi sub-machine gun.

It was four or five hundred yards from the gates to the big house, the home of the Don. By the time Luigi barked his instructions to his troops the alarm was raised,

Leading about fifty of his men on foot up the drive, Luigi was met by a burst of fire from the front entrance of the house. This was countered by tossing a couple of hand grenades, one of which accurately hit the large doors and blew them open, dangling on their hinges. The other bounced off the wall, detonated and broke a lot of window glass.

As Luigi led the rush for the now open entrance he yelled to Angelo, "Take half the men and surround the house, kill any Corleoni you see!"

Luigi was armed with an old Thompson sub-machine gun fitted with a drum magazine holding one hundred .45 inch cartridges. A weapon he knew well from the old days.

He fired short bursts as he jogged up the stone steps, closely followed by his men, all equipped with Uzi sub-machine guns or Beretta automatic rifles. A forbidding bunch of desperados.

Once inside the building the attackers were met by a hail of bullets from at least a dozen sharpshooters, some on the stairs and balcony, others standing boldly on the ground floor.

The defenders were obviously taken by surprise as there was no coordinated shooting discipline. They were firing individually and desperately and were no match for Luigi's much larger squad of well prepared "soldiers" who wiped them out with cool efficiency and heavier fire power.

Under Luigi's orders the attackers searched all over the house and murdered every Corleoni they could find.

However, Luigi's personal luck ran out as he burst through a door into what was obviously a large family room. A man, later identified as the Don, opened fire with a machine-pistol and one heavy bullet hit Luigi in the abdomen just as he squeezed the trigger of his Thompson gun, the short burst blowing his assailant backward, dead as a doornail.

Luigi collapsed to the floor, groaning in agony at the terrible pain of his wound, his Thompson gun dropping as his grip loosened involuntarily.

"Get Angelo Rizzoli, quick," yelled a "soldier" as he hastened to help Luigi. Someone raced outside the building to find Angie who, with his men, was circling the house and shooting any Corleoni who tried to escape through the back doors and windows.

On hearing the news Angie wasted no time in getting to his wounded boss. As the firing slowly subsided and the body count rapidly rose Angie shouted to his men, "You, you and you," pointing to three men as he barked his instructions, "Find a bedroom, grab a mattress and get it here pronto."

The trio soon returned, placed the mattress beside their recumbent boss and heard Angie's next order, " Now, altogether, we will lift Don Luigi very gently on to the mattress, very gently remember."

They did this in unison successfully and Angie followed up with, "Now I want six men to carry the Don out side, down the steps carefully while you," pointing at another lad, " Run to the gates and tell the *consigliere* to send back the small van immediately."

There was still shooting in the gate area but the youngster did as he was told and the small van returned quickly.

Luigi was carefully put on board with two men to watch him, equipped with torn up sheets to wipe his perspiring face, forehead and stem the blood from his abdomen.

Angie drove to the gates and called the *consigliere* over. "Have you taken any prisoners." he queried. "There's two slightly wounded in the guard-house," was the reply.

"Bring me one who can walk," said Angie. This was done and a frightened young man looked fitfully at Angelo, convinced he was going to be killed, if not tortured.

"Have you got a doctor in this goddamned town?" Angie barked.

"Yes sir, yes sir," babbled the youngster.

" You are going to take us to the doctor by the shortest route and if you bungle the job you will meet a nasty end," rasped Angie savagely, continuing, "Now get in the front of this van beside me and tell me exactly where to drive."

Angie nodded to a listening "soldier" and told him, "Get in beside him and if I give you the word shoot him in the guts."

Hearing these words the white faced young prisoner's face turned even whiter.

Angie ordered two truckloads of his men to escort him and took off. There was desultory shooting in all directions so the wounded Luigi was transported to his fate under gunfire. Luckily, Angie's guide directed him to a clinic well out of the battle zone where there was more than one surgeon used to dealing with gunshot wounds. However they were not used to the arrival of a gun-toting Angelo Rizzoli threatening mayhem thus, "Get some people outside to bring in our Don for immediate attention, he's been shot in the guts by your Don and you are to drop whatever you are doing and concentrate on your new problem. And do it right or you all will be as dead as your Don."

The clinic staff had heard the extensive gunfire in the town but the surgeons had not expected to be treating one of the enemy!

However, Luigi was stretchered in and treated by the surgical staff under the observant eyes of Angie.

The senior surgeon hopefully told Angie,"We've done all we can for the patient. We have alleviated the pain as far as we are able at this time. May we suggest the patient is taken to Palermo Hospital as quickly as possible?"

Angelo thanked the surgeons with reluctant gruffness in his voice and added, "Put the patient in your best ambulance attended by your best orderly and we will escort our Don to Palermo. Two of our men will be in the ambulance beside your driver and two more will be in with your orderly, guarding the patient."

These orders were obeyed with great alacrity and the ambulance soon rumbled away escorted by two truckloads of "soldiers" controlled by Angie.

Angie stopped briefly at the gates to the big house where all firing had ceased. "Burn the house and everything in it," he ordered, "And bring our few wounded men to Palermo Hospital before heading for home."

There was no problem at Palermo where Angie learned that Luigi's abdominal wound was very serious. So serious, in fact, that if he did not receive ultra-sophisticated treatment rapidly he would be dead within a couple of weeks. The surgical staff at Palermo were united in stating that the best people to attend to Luigi's case were at St. Thomas's Hospital in London, UK.

Angie thought fast. He 'phoned me in Montreal and told me the situation, suggesting that Firdaussi and I should get to England pronto and contact St. Thomas's. We agreed and moved over the Atlantic with all haste.

Our colleague then chartered a hospital jet from Rome to be flown to Palermo to pick up Luigi.

Angie and half a dozen "soldiers" stayed with his boss until this occurred, then sent the warriors back to their manor in East Sicily under the command of the *consigliere* and joined the para-medics in the aircraft.

All this activity could only take place by spending a lot of money. Luckily our mob members had plenty of this commodity which is known to the un-lucky as "filthy lucre" for some reason!

* * * * *

Ferdaussi and I met Angie at the Dorchester Hotel in London, England and ensured that Luigi received the best available treatment from the internationally famous surgeons at St. Thomas's Hospital. We had also arranged for Tania, Luigi's wife to fly to London accompanied by Angelo's wife Maria. We all had accommodation in the Dorchester Hotel.

Naturally, Tania was eager to visit her spouse and these visits improved his morale during his bouts of suffering.

Having a very tough constitution helped Luigi to respond favorably to his skilled surgical treatment to the degree that after a couple of weeks his doctors stated that he was out of danger and could be moved to a more convivial environment. Here he was ordered to rest and recuperate.

By mutual consent I telephoned the butler at Cottingham Hall and instructed him that Mr. Ferraro and his wife would be arriving shortly for a prolonged stay. In addition Mr. Rizzoli and his wife plus Firdaussi and me would also be staying for an indeterminate period.

I emphasized that Luigi was recuperating from serious surgery and needed a bedroom suitable for visits from doctors and medical staff.

We arranged that Luigi would be transported to Cottingham Hall in a special ambulance, tended by para-medics and with Angelo as passenger for security reasons.

I ordered Fred Pierce, the head chauffeur at Cottingham Hall to pick our gang up at the Dorchester Hotel in one of the Rolls-Royce sedans; timing it so that our departure coincided with Luigi's ambulance trip from the hospital. Another security precaution allowing us to keep an eye on the ambulance as it traveled south.

Everything was organized for us on arrival at Cottingham Hall. Luigi was carried to his room by the para-medics and we made ourselves comfortable before partaking of a good lunch.

The ambulance departed and after lunch we got down to discussing our future business aspects.

* * * * *

Luigi had recovered sufficiently to take part in our discussion and, in fact opened with the statement, "We still know nothing about who killed Otto Guynemer. For all we know they may intend to knock off all of us in their own good time."

This remark merely added strength to our own thoughts on the subject. We had all been involved in the killing game on numerous occasions but this time we could well be the targets not the executioners. A sobering situation indeed!

I remembered how Luigi, many years ago, had warned me that "Once you're in the mob you are in for keeps. The only way out is in a coffin!"

Hence I was very surprised when Luigi, the boss of our mob, suggested, " I guess we've all done pretty well out of the rackets and it could be the right time to retire and let new boys take over." Adding after a pause to let us get over the shock, " I've been thinking since the doc. pulled the slug out of my belly that a few years living here at Cottingham with my wife Tania would be a good finish to a hectic existence. I appreciate that the Cottingham estate belongs to all of us and, of course, you guys can come and go as you please or even live here yourselves, there's enough goddamn room for an army!"

We chuckled at the last remark until Angie stepped in with, "What about Sicily, boss, and the drug racket?"

Luigi pondered for long seconds before answering, "We have just knocked hell out of the Corleoni mob, their Don was killed with quite a lot of his "soldiers" and this shoot-out should keep them quiet for a bit. As you all know," Luigi looked around at us with a grin before continuing, "As you all know we beat them into the ground once before and they recovered. They will recover from this recent attack and life for our mob in Sicily will be one long fire fight. That's why I reckon this is a good time to retire and enjoy life in another country."

We spent hours chewing things over and working out the best methods to hand over our intricate drug and vice rackets to the next guys in line. We discovered that retiring from our sophisticated organization appeared to be quite complicated! Also there was hell of a lot of money involved!

* * * * *

CHAPTER TWENTY-ONE

ADIEU ANGELO RIZZOLI

It was decided primarily that Firdaussi and I would undertake the task of traveling around our criminal circuit to inform the lads and lasses in charge of each area that they were from now on the actual big bosses, no longer under our control and supervision.

This information would please most of them but they would have to learn to co-operate with the other area bosses in the chain to keep the flow of narcotics running at practical levels. On the other hand they would all make a lot more money because our Good Ol' Boys would be giving up our cut of the pelf.

As I remarked to my colleagues, "Knowing the guys we are dealing with there is bound to be a power struggle between one or two ambitious merchants who aim to be *capo di tutto capi* (boss of all bosses). So I doubt if things will go perfectly smoothly when we quit."

"So what?" queried Luigi, "They've had things easy under our control. Let them learn to adapt and if they have to struggle they will learn the hard way just as we did in the past."

Firdaussi made her usual common-sense addition to the discussion with, "I feel we have to spend some time with our local bosses to put them in the picture about the whole narcotics operation that we have built up over the years. Much of the racket was under our personal supervision and if these guys aren't informed of those functions controlled by us they will feel out of their depth and insecure. For instance, none of these guys know about organizing our cargo ship to and from Montreal with drug shipments. Without this kind of knowledge the system could degenerate into separate gangs with the ambitious guys seeking more power. This will mean gang wars and shooting. And that will mean nosey cops from a dozen different countries being involved and learning a lot about the system. They may even find clues concerning our involvement. What kind of retirement will it be for us guys if a bunch of high-powered detectives are on our trail?" Firdaussi ceased her lecture, broke off a piece of a chocolate bar and popped it in her mouth, seeming to suggest with this gesture that she had said her piece and was waiting for comments.

"You sure made some good points, Firdy," said Luigi and we all echoed his remark.

I broke in with a feeble effort at humor, "I guess we'll have to print a handbook entitled "The Good Ol' Boys Global Drug Distribution System," sub-titled "How To Run It Successfully!" and hand out copies to all the guys involved.

There were a few titters at my disclosure but nothing more!

Angelo added that, "Firdaussi's remarks make sense and I guess when she and Deac make the rounds they will ensure that the area bosses get all the information and contacts necessary to avoid the breakdown of the drug racket."

We all agreed that this was essential and must be done.

* * * * *

Luigi was still convalescing from his nasty stomach wound which was greatly improved but gave him occasional pain and discomfort.

However he was determined to arrange a new boss to take his place in his Sicilian family.

Thinking I was stating the obvious I suggested that his son Roberto could take over in natural succession as head of the family. As I spoke I thought I detected a faint smile in my direction from Angelo and I vaguely wondered why.

Luigi appreciated my interest in the affair but took great pains to describe his problem, thus, "Deac, the traditional mafia system does not permit the capo of a family to indulge in...," He halted briefly and queried, "What the hell is that word, neput, nopit...?" I helped him out with, "Nepotism, Luigi." and he carried on, "We don't allow nepotism, Deac, the retiring capo or boss is not permitted under the ancient Cosa Nostra rules to pick the new boss.

It must be done by a common vote under the guidance of the *consigliere* and the senior *capodecine*."

I acknowledged Luigi's explanation by a couple of nods and realized why Angelo, the born mafioso had smiled. I then asked, "What plans have you in mind for your son Roberto, Luigi?"

"He's well able to make his own mind up concerning his future moves, Deac, but as I have no wish to see him tangled with that goddamned Corleoni mob and an ever possible bloody end to his life I intend to use my influence to get him to leave Sicily. As you know, Deac, I managed to fix his attendance at Cambridge University in UK where he graduated with honors and then in USA at Massachusetts Institute of Technology where he got a degree in management science. So he's well educated and trained in business management. On top of which he has served in senior executive positions in two or three major commercial organizations in USA and UK.

What I had in mind, Deac, was to put him in charge of our company Pharos International Corporation which, as you know, is based and registered in London, UK. As you and Angelo are equal owners of Pharos with me I would naturally require your agreement before approaching Roberto."

"Well, Luigi," I began, "You've got my agreement right now and," I eyed Angelo, "I doubt if Angie has any objections to your scheme, have you Angie?"

Angie nodded vigorously, "I agree absolutely, I think it's a damn good idea," he added.

I reminded my colleagues that our old friend and fellow mobster, Abdul Mahmoud, still based in Cairo, Egypt was also part owner of Pharos International Corporation. I was sure he would agree because during a recent telephone conversation he had hinted that he was contemplating retirement with a view to living in England with his wife Chantal. Their two sons, now adult and successful in business both lived in UK so they would not be lonely. I agreed to contact Abdul and get his OK to Luigi's plan for Roberto.

Our discussion ended by Luigi telling Angelo that he wanted him to return to Sicily and supervise the election of a new boss of the Ferraro family, at the same time asking Roberto to visit his father at Cottingham Hall right away. Firdaussi and I were to start planning our international round trip to inform our cohorts in many countries that they were now on their own as our Sicilian cartel was quitting.

Not an envious task for us although Firdy, with her usual sangfroid, stated "We'll make a good vacation of it, Deac, and live expensively!"

* * * * *

Angelo and spouse Maria left for Sicily after informing Roberto, nominally the family boss, of their time of arrival.

They were picked up in Syracuse by a senior capodecina and rapidly transported by car to the family manor where they were welcomed by Luigi's son Roberto before retiring to their own nearby residence. Here they had a good clean up and meal before relaxing after their rather hurried journey.

At a later discussion Roberto informed Angelo that the decimated Corleoni mob were uttering fearful threats against Luigi's family so all the many members, male and female had to be on the alert permanently. As Luigi had mentioned earlier life in Sicily was going to be a perpetual gun-fight. Not a comfortable situation.

Angelo mentioned to Roberto, "Your father would like you to visit him in England to talk about your future. I'll look after things here while you are away and you'll find Luigi is getting over his bullet wound in fine style. He was lucky he wasn't killed but we managed to get him to the hospital promptly in spite of the battle that was raging in Corleone."

Roberto smiled as he replied,"Thanks to you Angie; you risked your neck looking after my father and I thank you for it. It was your rapid response that saved his life. Any delay and the surgeons couldn't have saved him, that's for sure."

Roberto paused briefly, then, "You are very close to my father, Angie, can you drop me a hint what he will suggest about my future?"

Angie gave a mischievous grin and said laughingly, "Roberto, you are well aware that true Sicilians know how to keep their mouths shut and I am a born Sicilian. However, as you are the son of our family boss I intend to look upon your comment as an order! So I'll drop you a hint as you commanded! You are aware that our company Pharos International Corporation is owned by us senior members? Well, we have all agreed with your father to offer you the executive president position of Pharos. Should you accept, Roberto, you will be given a sizeable share holding in the company which will doubtless increase as time marches on.

So that's it, Roberto," grinned Angelo, " Just don't tell Luigi that I spilled the beans to you."

Roberto laughed in response, adding," I'll look surprised when he makes the offer, Angie, but..." and here he paused, becoming serious, " surely if I accept this offer I will be based in London, England and be traveling world-wide to visit and control the many company branches? Will that be acceptable to the family in Sicily?"

"You know," replied Angelo, "that I have been ordered to return here to organize the election of a capo to take over from your father, who is now intending to retire. So your absence will not only be acceptable to the new regime but will probably be welcomed by the new boss as it will avoid any possible embarrassment caused by your constant presence, looming like the shadow of the past over the new set-up!"

Roberto smiled as he responded, " I would try hard not to loom, Angie, although I must admit that you have made a very convincing argument in favor of my leaving Sicily."

With that remark the discussion tailed off and Roberto invited Angelo and his spouse Maria to join him for dinner in the big house intimating at the same time that he would be leaving to visit his father in England the next morning.

* * * * *

Roberto was picked up at London Heathrow Airport by chauffeur Fred Pierce and shuttled to Cottingham Hall in a Rolls Royce limo.

He found Luigi, his father, looking a bit strained as he was still convalescing from the dangerous bullet wound in his abdomen. However, Luigi acted in his usual ebullient fashion and welcomed his son and heir enthusiastically.

Firdaussi and I were still at Cottingham Hall enjoying the fruits of life on an English country estate even though we were ostensibly planning our international world tour to negate control of our vast drug and vice rackets. After all we were legally part owners of that large and ancient estate so we were entitled to enjoy it!

We joined Luigi, his wife Tania and Roberto for lunch, superb cuisine as usual, and all lounged together afterwards in the adjacent antechamber sipping our coffees and brandy while we chatted about this and that.

It was not long before Luigi, with a sly nod to Firdy and I, broached the subject of Roberto's future. Of course we were not aware that Angelo had tipped off Roberto about the proposal to offer him executive control of Pharos International Corporation so his reaction appeared normal.

He was a good actor and gave the appearance of being surprised at the offer. His mind must have been made up in advance as, after some discussion and many questions, he accepted, which pleased his father and his mother Tania enormously.

As Luigi was still recuperating from his bullet wound it fell to me to get Roberto installed as boss of Pharos International Corporation. This meant a sojourn in London for Firdy and I where we would have to attend meetings with the current board of directors at Pharos headquarters and consultation with company attorneys. This job had to be performed effectively and above all, legally.

There was also the question of applying for British nationality or at least permanent residence in UK for Luigi, Tania and Roberto. I had a feeling that members of a Sicilian Cosa Nostra family would not be welcomed with open arms by the British Immigration authority. However that problem could be sorted out later. The first thing was to get Roberto installed in Pharos. As Firdy and I were part owners in this impressive international organization we had a lot of weight to throw around in our negotiations.

* * * * *

Meanwhile Angelo was busily organizing the election of the next Don of the Ferraro family in Sicily. Actually there was virtually no competition in this so-called election. The mass of family members entitled to vote were unanimous in their choice.

The man chosen was Enrico Campagna, long time *consigliere* to Luigi and a leader of the Sicilian mafia resistance fighters against the German invaders in World War Two.

Angelo had expected this result and, as Luigi's representative, laid on a ceremonial take-over by Enrico as the new Don. A traditional occasion which impressed the family and cemented Enrico's new status.

It was agreed that the new regime should be "legalized" by informing the Cosa Nostra Commission of the change in leadership. There was a branch of the Commission at Syracuse, a city not far from the Ferraro family manor so Angelo volunteered to visit them and inform them of the new regime. Enrico Campagna agreed and told Angelo, "Take a couple of our soldiers with you, Angie, remember those Corleoni bastards have just about run the Commission for their own ends."

To which Angelo replied somewhat jocularly, " After our last battle with that mob I doubt they have enough men left to influence the Commission. Don't forget, Enrico, that Luigi knocked off their boss personally and you and I saw a hell of a lot of bodies that weren't moving!"

"True, Angie," said Enrico, "I guess with your experience you won't be visiting the Commission with your eyes shut, just be careful."

So Angelo arranged to meet the Commission in two days time and decided to take Maria, his spouse, with him and enjoy the attractions of Syracuse, a lively and historic city, while having a little sophisticated relaxation after completing the Commission business.

* * * * *

Angelo and Maria were driven to Syracuse on the due date by one of the family soldiers. This young man was under direct orders from the new family Don, Enrico Campagna, to guard

Angelo and Maria with his life if necessary. However, after speaking to the Commission, Angelo told the soldier to drive back home as he and Maria were going to see the sights and stay the night at the Hotel Sicilia.

"Tell the Don that we will find our own way back tomorrow and not to worry about our safety," said Angie with a laugh. So the young man took off for home somewhat reluctantly and left our couple to see a show and look for a decent night club where they could spend an enjoyable evening.

They soon found what they wanted when an obliging cab driver directed them to the Omar Khayyam night club, telling them, "This is the classiest joint in Syracuse, the food is mouth-watering and the belly-dancers are out of this world, but it's gonna cost you plenty!"

Angie grinned at this information because in her younger days his spouse Maria was noted for her belly-dancing ability

He gave Maria a knowing nudge as he told the cabbie, "Take us there quick as you like, we're hungry and would like to see the dancers!"

They soon arrived at the Omar Khayyam, paid the cabbie, entered and were escorted to a front row table. They ordered dinner and aperitives, sitting back comfortably to enjoy both food and show.

Unfortunately their enjoyment did not last more than five minutes.

Unseen by either, three men entered the busy club and walked rapidly to their table. Two of the men pulled twin barrel sawn-off shotguns from under their jackets and opened fire immediately on Angelo and Maria. As the heavy buckshot slugs ripped into their bodies they were blasted off their chairs, stone dead before they knew what had hit them.

The third assailant had drawn a .45 Colt pistol and gave each victim the *coup de grace* bullet in the head.

The gunmen looked around the shocked club warningly as if to suggest, "Open your mouths and you'll get the same!" before walking off unhurriedly through the doors to their get-away car.

* * * * *

CHAPTER TWENTY-TWO

Who's Next?

News of the sudden slaying of Angelo and his wife Maria came as a shock to his old confederates; those of us who were left, that is!

It was obvious to all of us that the executioners were Corleoni gunmen and expert ones at that. Someone must have tipped off the Corleoni family that Angie and his spouse were going to visit Syracuse. The killers had probably followed their intended victims from the moment they left the Commission building and decided that the Omar Khayyam night club was the ideal killing zone.

We were somewhat surprised that Angelo, a highly experienced gunman himself, should have been finally caught out in such a blatant manner. Still, the old proverb states that, "He who lives by the sword, dies by the sword." The only difference was that the sword had changed to sawn-off shotguns.

"Will you go to Sicily for the funerals, Deac?" queried Luigi, "And make sure Angie and Maria have a good send off?"

"Sure I will," I replied, having guessed that this requirement would be broached.

" I would go myself,"added Luigi, "but the goddamned doctor won't let me walk too far."

I was not very keen to visit Sicily for the funerals because past history proved that many an assassination had occurred during funeral processions and services.

It was obvious that the Corleoni mob would be well aware of the date and time of the ceremony and it would not be difficult to spot the senior mourners in attendance.

I, of course, would be a senior mourner and a potential target for a sniper. Not a happy situation!

However I had agreed to go and it was consoling to know that we would be protected by our own "soldier" bodyguards.

Naturally, funeral or no funeral, I would be carrying a suitable pistol as my last line of defense. I trusted our bodyguards, of course, but I trusted myself more!

Ferdaussi insisted on coming to Sicily with me in spite of my natural precautionary objections. I was glad really as it's always good for moral when you have a companion that you trust and rely on completely.

We went through all the appropriate motions on the day and gave Angelo and Maria a good send off as Luigi had suggested. I was more than relieved to live through the funeral ceremony and not be involved in a shoot out.

At the end of a somewhat tiresome and worrying formal occasion Firdaussi and I gave a polite and rapid farewell to the new Don and headed for Syracuse airport by road at high speed, escorted by half a dozen "soldiers" in a follow up car.

We did not tarry at the airport as we had ordered a private charter aircraft to fly us to Rome.

At Rome we had a substantial and welcome dinner at the top hotel where we stayed the night before taking off for London in the morning.

* * * * *

Once we landed at Heathrow London Airport we went through our usual routine. Fred Pierce, the ancient chauffeur, picked us up in one of his Rolls-Royce limos and ferried us to Cottingham Hall with his usual calm rapidity.

Luigi and Tania were pleased to see us again and listened eagerly to our description of the funeral.

" So none of those Corleoni scum took a shot at you, Deac?" said Luigi, more as a remark than a query.

He smiled when I replied, " Firdaussi and I were both tooled up so we were ready for a little gun play even though it never happened, Luigi."

Luigi's reply was to the point. "I hope the occasion never happens again, Deac; we are all getting a bit too old for this gun-slinging caper and just a little bit slower, I guess."

We all acknowledged our agreement with this statement coincidentally with the advent of the butler who announced that dinner was ready. So we stubbed our smokes and traipsed our way into the dining room. We traipsed rather than marched because Luigi had to totter along because of his belly wound which still caused him some discomfort when he moved.

Our discussion continued during dinner and it was decided that now Luigi's son Roberto was due to be installed as head of Pharos International Corporation, Firdaussi and I should leave for London next day and control the negotiations involved. We had already informed the company lawyers of our intentions so the legal measures should be sorted out rapidly.

There was the problem of obtaining British citizenship for Luigi, Tania and Roberto now they had decided to live permanently at Cottishall. I suggested they would have little difficulty with the Immigration department considering they were respectable Italian citizens with clean criminal records! On viewing the mish-mash of immigrants being accepted by Immigration our two applicants, wealthy business people who would never be a drain on the British tax payer, would be highly desirable. Especially if they donated liberally to the political party in power!

And so it turned out eventually. A top Cosa Nostra mobster and his ex-prostitute lady wife lived a life of genteel elegance in a large country estate in Sussex, England. With almost unlimited drug and vice engendered funds they were modestly generous to employees and local villagers alike. An example to all!

* * * * *

Firdaussi and I were driven up to London and booked in at the Dorchester's top suite. As Firdaussi remarked, "We're doing an important job so we need up-market bed and breakfast!"

A series of meetings with top management and the company attorneys soon settled Roberto in Pharos International as chairman of the board of directors. We insisted he was also installed as chief executive officer thus ensuring he was the boss and had complete control of the company. As Firdaussi and I were major part owners of the company and acting for the other owners we had the punch needed to get what we wanted.

We let Luigi know that we had successfully completed our mission and set off by chartered jet to Montreal, Canada.

* * * * *

We discussed our future as we sped en route to Canada. It was intended that we would inform our numerous cohorts in the drug and vice rackets that they were no longer under our control.

This should please them because they would now be the big bosses in their areas and would no longer have to pay us our cut of the proceeds. So they would be much wealthier as our cut was rather large!

However, as Firdy had stated previously, we had to make sure they knew our complicated drug distribution system in Europe, Canada, USA and the Caribbean otherwise they could suddenly find themselves out of work. And unemployed mobsters can cause gang wars and other troubles which could involve top cops of many countries. We did not want any of these top cops discovering leads to our cartel, the Good Ol' Boys!

Even though we were on the verge of retirement.

* * * * *

So after settling comfortably in our Montreal residence we made a point of contacting Nicolo Rizzoli asking him to a meal at our favourite restaurant.

He accepted eagerly and came with his wife. We put him in the picture about the deaths of Otto and Angelo but little more. He was surprised and gratified to learn that we were handing over complete control of the Canadian drug racket and that he now really was the big local boss. We explained who was now running our cargo boat loads of dope from Europe and indicated that he should meet with these people and make a workable relationship.

He was told nothing of our future plans as we intended to

sever our relationship with gangland completely. After our meal we sent Nicolo and his wife home no doubt with the slightly uncomfortable feeling that he was no longer under the overall protection of our powerful Sicilian cartel. However, from what we read in the media at later dates, Nicolo's family soon basked in the spotlight as the Mafia bosses of Montreal.

* * * * *

CHAPTER TWENTY-THREE

CASHING IN

We arranged a meeting with the senior executives of Pharos International Corporation branch in Montreal to put them in the picture about the new Chairman/Chief Executive Officer in London headquarters.

Roberto intended to visit the Montreal branch at the earliest opportunity but had asked us to let the senior executives be forewarned by us in person.

We decided to sell our Montreal house as well as the near-by house of Angelo and Maria. They wouldn't be needing it any more. These transactions were put in the hands of our previous realtor, the guy who had sold them to us originally.

Then we took off for our tour and visited our old drug contacts in Miami, Aruba and Nicaragua to put them in the picture. That is about all we did. Nothing was mentioned about our future plans and if anyone insisted on being told they were handed a lot of intentional falsehoods! Keep them happy was our motto! We also sold even more of our property during our visits.

We did not intend to visit Europe to pass on the information concerning the new system. Pasquale Mangano, our helicopter expert had finished his job of training new helicopter pilots to aid the Bikers in British Columbia so we asked him, and paid him well, to tell our contacts in Marseilles and Paris, France, that we were no longer their bosses. As he was frequently flying dope from Corsica to Marseilles and Paris he knew the chief guys in both areas and was willing to do what we required. At the same time the boss in Corsica would be put in the picture. As an extra reward we arranged that Pasquale would be given the deeds of our residence in Corsica, very up-market, so he could sell it or live in it with his wife and family.

* * * * *

Firdy and I, after long discussion, decided the best place for us to live and settle down after our hectic criminal careers was Canada. Also probably the safest place!

So we applied to become citizens of the Great Frozen North and discovered that Immigration might allow us, if our credentials were valid, to become official Permanent Residents, not Canadian Citizens. The latter might be possible after a further three year wait.

All very tedious but we were not in a great hurry as we intended to enjoy life at our newly found leisure.

So while Immigration was processing us at harebrained speed (?) we explored the Canadian West for a suitable home. We chose British Columbia because we guessed the weather and climate were somewhat more temperate than points east.

Eventually we bought an excellent estate, overlooking the coast, near Qualicum Beach on Vancouver Island. We enjoyed the peace and quiet for a time and for variety hopped over to Vancouver by air.

However, the peace and quiet was too much for our lively dispositions to tolerate so we sold up and headed south for Victoria, the capital of B.C. Here we bought a beautiful house and acreage in the Oak Bay area and are living there yet.

Victoria gives us everything we need, first-class restaurants, as much art and culture as we can stand plus the ability to pop over to Washington State, USA, and enjoy similar facilities in Seattle.

I am the only survivor of the original Cairo group which I joined so long ago.

Luigi died naturally when he reached ninety years of age. Otto Guynemer was shot down at ninety years. Angelo Rizzoli was shot to death in Sicily and Abdul Mahmoud died in Egypt, aged eighty-two.

I am now ninety-one and Firdaussi's eighty-eight, both living the good life after careers of earnest endeavor!

END

APPENDIX A

CHARACTERS

Otto Guynemer	The Big Boss
Luigi Ferraro	Mafioso, American gangster, No.2 Boss
Abdul Mahmoud	Arab, Cairo gangster
Deacon Roy	Joined mob 1938 and rose to top rank
Firdaussi	Wife of Deacon Roy
Tania	Wife of Luigi Ferraro
Angelo Rizzoli	Mafioso, American gangster
Maria	Wife of Angelo Rizzoli
Chantelle	French wife of Abdul Mahmoud
Pasquale Mangano	Helicopter pilot, Corsican Mafioso
Santos Salvatore	Mafia Boss, Florida, USA
Carlos Mancini	Mafia Boss, Louisiana, USA
Jo Fratello	Mafia Boss, Chicago, USA
JFK	John F Kennedy,President USA
Jack Rubenstein	Jack Ruby, racketeer, Dallas, Texas
Oswald, Lee Harvey	Accused of JFK assassination
John Connally	Governor of Texas. Shot in Dallas
Joseph Bonnano	Boss of New York Cosa Nostra family
Vincenzo Cotillo	Mafia Boss in Montreal, Canada
Nicolo Rizzoli	Mafia Boss in Montreal, Canada

APPENDIX A (continued)
CHARACTERS

Bernardo Pacelli	Boss of Corleone mafia family Sicily
Fred Pierce	Chauffeur at Guynemer's Cottingham Hall
Louis Gratto	Underboss to Vincenzo Cotillo, Montreal
Enrico Campagna	Senior member of Luigi's mafia family
Paolo Velio	Underboss to Vincenzo Cotillo, Montreal
Giuseppa	Wife of Nicolo Rizzolo
John Norris	Executive of Pharos International Co.
Dr. Albert Klesinger	Money launderer in Liechtenstein
Meyer Lansky	Jewish financial adviser to Cosa Nostra
Flavio Velio	Brother of Paolo Velio
Pietro Caselli	Friend and adviser to Paolo Velio
Roderigo Sanchez	Miami agent of Colombian drug cartel
Pablo Escobar-Gavira	Boss of Colombian drug cartel
Gerard Fenlac	French air charter company boss, Paris
Joseph Profaci	Montreal mafia restaurant manager
Dwain Jackson	Bikers Boss in BC and Washington State
Chief Inspector Gates	Detective investigating Guynemer's death
Detective Sgt Philips	Aiding Chief Inspector Gates
Roberto Ferraro	Son of Luigi and Tania Ferraro

APPENDIX B

Chronological Synopsis

Progress To Infamy:

1907 Young Luigi sent to USA from Sicily by mafia father, Don Ferraro

1923 Otto Guynemer moved to USA. Worked with Al Capone

1929 The St. Valentine's Day Massacre, Chicago USA. Suspected involvement of Guynemer and Luigi Ferraro

1930 Guynemer quit Chicago. Surveyed Middle East prospects

1930 Luigi Ferraro returned to his mafia family in Sicily

1931 Guynemer set up drug and vice business with Luigi Ferraro in Cairo, Egypt

1932 Abdul Mahmoud, Arab gangster, joined Guynemer and Luigi Ferraro in Cairo

1938 Deacon Roy's first contact with the mob in Cairo

1939 The Palestine fire-fight

1939 The Alexandria Massacre

1940 The Sicilian Bombing

1940 The Lebanon Battle

1940 The Ar Ramadi Battle

1942 Luigi's father murdered in Sicily by German SS officer

1943 Luigi visits Sicily to avenge father's death

APPENDIX B (continued)

Progress to Infamy

1943 Sicilian Vespers for the Schutzstaffel in Sicily

1945 Guynemer sells Middle East business and distributes loot

1946 Guynemer returns to England.

1946 Deacon and Firdaussi visit Guynemer in England

1947 Deacon and Firdaussi buy home in Corsica

1948 Don Luigi's wife Tania gives birth to a son

1948 Marseilles, France, visited to evaluate the situation

1950 The Marseilles Massacre

1952 Brothel chain established in southern France

1953 Cottingham Hall Revels

1953 The Paris Massacre

1954 Drug distribution and vice racket organized in France

1955 Mob began to open up Europe for drug and vice business

1960 The Camorra Massacre

1961 European drug and vice system well established

1961 The Good Ol' Boys asked to visit Miami USA

1962 Drug shipments sold to Cosa Nostra USA

1962 Deacon Roy and Firdaussi visit USA to check distribution

1963 The Good Ol' Boys invited to assassinate JFK

www.ingramcontent.com/pod-product-compliance
Ingram Content Group UK Ltd.
Pitfield, Milton Keynes, MK11 3LW, UK
UKHW020141250726
13967UKWH00002B/790

9 781425 185152